OTHERWORLD
VOLUME ONE
TALES

YASMINE
NEW YORK TIMES BESTSELLING AUTHOR
GALENORN

A Nightqueen Enterprises LLC Publication
Published by Yasmine Galenorn
PO Box 2037, Kirkland WA 98083-2037

Cover Design by Earthly Charms
Cover Art: Tony Mauro (copyright-Yasmine Galenorn)

A Nightqueen Enterprises, LLC Publication
Published in the United States of America

ACKNOWLEDGMENTS & INTRODUCTION

When I first started writing WITCHLING twelve years ago, I had no clue that the series would become so popular. It amazed me how much my readers took to the Sisters, and how rapidly the series gained traction. Nineteen books later, I'm finishing the series on my own and writing short pieces and novelettes on the side. This volume contains three of the e-collections that I put out a couple years ago: TALES FROM OTHERWORLD, MEN OF OTHERWORLD, COLLECTION 1, and MEN OF OTHERWORLD, COLLECTION 2. I'm putting it out in print and e-format form for those who want all of the short stories together. Another volume will follow next year containing some of the other novellas that I've released in indie.

I'm so grateful to my readers who've followed me this far. To the ones who've remained like glue to the adventures of the sisters—thank you for the love you've given this world of mine, and all my worlds. I hope you enjoy the side stories—which I intend to continue writing.

Thanks also go to my husband, Samwise, who has been my biggest supporter as I've shifted my career to the indie side. And thanks to my friends who have cheered me on—especially Jo and Carol. Thank you to my assistants Jenn and Andria for all their help. And thank you to my fellow authors in my UF group, who have helped me learn what I needed to learn in order to take my career into my own hands.

A most reverent nod to my spiritual guardians—Mielikki, Tapio, Ukko, Rauni, and the Lady Brighid. They guide my life, and my heart.

And of course, love and scritches to my fuzzy brigade—Caly, Brighid, Morgana, and little boy Apple. I would be lost without my cats.

Bright Blessings, and for more information about all my work, please see my website at Galenorn.com, and sign up for my newsletter.

Bright Blessings,
~The Painted Panther~
~Yasmine Galenorn~

TABLE OF CONTENTS

Part One

Tales From Otherworld

Naked as a Moon Witch

This story takes place after the D'Artigo Sisters come Earthside, but before Witchling starts. Camille's referred to this incident a number of times, and I thought it would be fun to explore just what happened...

SOMETIMES, BEING A Witch just didn't pay. And the fact that my magic backfired half the time meant that some days, it was barely tolerable...

It was a week like any other, with no customers coming by. Usually The Indigo Crescent, my bookstore, did a fairly steady business, but for once it had been sunny in Seattle, and everybody was out skateboarding and hanging in the parks. Nobody wanted to be cooped up in a dusty little bookstore. By three PM, I was hot, and tired, and so bored out of my mind that I couldn't stand it, when it occurred to me that I could occupy myself by trying out some of the spells that kept backfiring on me. Nothing offensive of course. I didn't want to blow a hole in the wall, that much I was certain of.

So, I decided to try a spell that I'd been working on for several years, but that I could never manage to cast. Nothing ever happened when I tried—just a fizzle and spurt, and boom, nada. I didn't need any components, either, which was another plus. Without further ado, I retreated to the back hall and focused, whispering the charm.

By the powers of three times three,
By cape and cloak, by breast and knee,
Let others lose their powers to see me.

I waited. *Nothing*. I looked at my hand. *Still there*. Great, another failure. With a sigh, I headed back to the front of the shop and started shelving another box of used books that I'd bought off a starving college student.

About twenty minutes later, a young guy entered the shop, complete with requisite Birkenstocks and backpack. He headed toward the science fiction section without looking at me. A moment later, apparently unable to find what he wanted, he turned around, about to ask for help. But the words died on his lips as he stood there, staring at me, eyes firmly planted on my boobs.

His jaw dropped and he started to stutter. No actual words came out of his mouth as he continued to stare at my breasts. Then, his eyes moved down to my crotch.

Oh fuck. I knew that I had an effect on men—you couldn't be half-Fae and not have an effect on humans. But this was a little much to take, even for me.

Irate, I marched over and, with my hands on hips, demanded, "What's the matter? Can't see my face?"

At that moment, Iris entered the shop. She gasped. "Camille!"

"Not now, Iris. I'm giving this young man a lesson in manners." Granted, he was about my age if you count everything relative, but that didn't matter. I had a good forty Earthside years on him and I wasn't about to put up with this bullshit.

"But Camille...?" Iris was sounding more urgent. She bustled behind the counter and grabbed my arm. "This can't wait. Can you please come over here? *Now?*"

Exasperated, I started to shake her off, but the look on her face stopped me. Whether it was absolute horror, or chagrin and embarrassment, I couldn't tell, but the house sprite was definitely on the edge of uncomfortable.

I let out a sigh and glanced at my voyeur. "Listen, you. Wait here."

He nodded, his gaze still glued to my chest. "Whatever you say." It was then that I noticed he was holding a very large book in front of his pants.

Growing more disgusted by the moment, I followed Iris to the back. The minute we reached my office, she pushed me through the door. And trust me, for someone who was barely 4'1" and who looked like the Swiss Miss Cocoa girl, she packed a punch when she wanted to.

"What is going on? Why are you acting so strange? I want that pervert out of here." I wasn't sure who I was more irritated at by now: the guy or Iris.

"You really think this is all his fault? Dressed like that?" She gave a little snort.

I glanced down. I was wearing my usual gear. Black rayon skirt. Purple bustier. Stiletto sandals. Yeah, it was sexy but so what? It wasn't like I was wearing a negligee.

"What are you talking about? I look perfectly respectable."

"Really? *Really*? Girl, I know you like to flaunt it but I never thought you were a closet nudist." Iris stared at me like I'd just tried to tell her that Santa didn't exist, when we both knew he did. For that matter, he was a freakshow scary-assed dude.

"Nudist?" Taken aback, I glanced down. "What the fuck are you talking about? Last time I looked in the dictionary, nudist didn't include an alternative definition for someone wearing clothes!"

Iris scrunched up her lips and cocked her head. "Um, Camille. In case you haven't noticed, you're naked. N-E-K-K-I-D."

What the hell? I glanced down at my clothes again. "No I'm not!" I went into a lengthy description of what I was wearing, but she stood there shaking her head.

"I don't see a thing. Except your massively round boobs and your Brazilian." She let out a laugh. "You are trying to tell me you have on a skirt, panties, and bustier?"

I grabbed her hand and brought it toward me. Her eyes narrowed like she was a rabbit heading directly toward a hawk, but then she let out a little 'oh' as her fingers came in contact with my skirt. She tugged on it.

"Oh, great gods. Camille, I can't see your skirt. I can't see any of your clothing! All I see is a lot of beautiful, pale skin." She followed the hem of the skirt and then touched my waist, feeling the lacings on the bustier. "What on earth have you been doing?"

I thought for a moment, and then it hit me. "Oh no! No...no...no! No wonder...that poor man out there! No wonder he couldn't stop..." I grabbed for a jacket off the coat rack but the minute I slipped it on, Iris let out a little cry.

"The jacket—it vanished! I can't see it now!"

Cripes! My spell must have backfired instead of fizzled out. I quickly told Iris what I'd done, and she started to laugh. I wanted to smack her one, but truth was, it sounded too funny, even to me.

"So now, all your clothes become invisible the minute you put them on! Oh Camille, you can't possibly stay here."

"I'm going to have to go home, but how do I get there? If I head out to my car, everybody will see me. I'm trapped!" Panicking now, and not sure at all how long the damned spell would last, I dropped into my office chair, blushing brighter than I had for years.

"It's a good thing that detective—Chase? It's a good thing he isn't here. He's been after your body for months." She frowned, tapping her toe as she contemplated the problem. "Here's what we'll do. You stay back here till after dark. Then, Mcnolly or Delilah will come get you and you can make a beeline into their car. You stay at home until this wears off. I'll take care of the bookstore."

"You'd do that? I know you're looking for work, but I didn't think you'd be interested in a bookstore. I thought you were looking for a family to bond with." Grateful for her help, I let out a sigh.

"I need something to do with my time while I look for a new family, so don't sweat it." She grinned at me. "Girl, your breasts are gorgeous."

I winked back and pointed at her chest. "Well, yours must give them a run for their money." The house sprite was pretty stacked, herself. "Anyway, yeah, that's the only option I have right now. If you could run upstairs, I think Delilah's in her office. But what about lover boy out there? I feel so bad now for yelling at him. What must he think?"

"I'll take care of him. Don't you worry about that. You just stay out of sight." As she headed back out to the front, I rubbed my head. Yeah, some days being a half-human, half-Fae witch just didn't live up to expectations.

It took me a week for the spell to wear off. After that, I decided to leave the invisibility up to anybody other than myself. After all, what's the use of having a closet filled with gorgeous clothes when nobody can see them?

An Otherworld Thanksgiving

This short, from Camille's point of view, takes place between the books Crimson Veil, moments before Priestess Dreaming starts. In fact, Priestess Dreaming begins on the tail end of this scene…

"WHERE ARE THE potatoes? We're going to need potatoes for tomorrow! Trillian, did you remember to pick them up?" Iris darted around Hanna, carrying a stockpot filled with soup for tonight's dinner. "And somebody better start the water for the eggs. If we don't get them boiled tonight, we won't have deviled eggs for canapés!"

Hanna lifted the pan of biscuits over her head. "Careful now, or we'll have no biscuits to go with the soup tonight!" She deftly maneuvered around Roz, who carried a bushel of apples over to the table for Delilah to peel. Apple pie was on the holiday menu, as well as the cherry pies that were about ready to come out of the oven. The smell in the kitchen was enough to set any mouth salivating.

Trillian grunted. "I got 'em. They're still out in the car. I'll run out and bring them in. Russets okay?"

"Perfect! While you're at it, can you dash over to my house and gather some basil, thyme, and parsley from the greenhouse? We need more than a few sprigs, mind you!" Iris flashed him a smile and he softened.

"You know I can't say no to you." And he was out the back door, into the blustery afternoon.

"Camille, are you done with the cherry pies yet?" Iris glanced my way and I felt like I should salute. We all knew Iris was running this show, with Hanna as her lieutenant commander, even though they did jostle over territory. The rest of us were just soldiers in the army, doing what we were told.

"I'm pulling them out of the oven right now." I bent down, carefully removing the cookie sheets from the rack. Two pies per sheet, there were eight in the big double oven. We had already baked eight pumpkin pies, and we'd make eight apple. With sixteen at the table tomorrow, including our new-found cousins, that would barely be enough to tide us through the weekend. We all had guerrilla appetites.

"Good then. I'll be back in a minute. I'm going to see if the tablecloths and napkins are dry yet." Iris bustled out of the kitchen, toward the laundry room.

"What about the turkey?" Morio was sitting at the table, next to Delilah, knife in hand. As she finished peeling the apples, he quickly sliced them into a bowl. Across from him, Menolly was arranging the slices in the pie plates. I felt for her this time of year. Even with the food-flavored blood, it had to suck not being able to join us in the feast.

"Smoky's supposed to bring the turkey. I asked him to go down to the store with Vanzir and pick out a twenty-five pounder. I don't know what could be keeping them." I frowned, glancing up at the clock. Surely, Smoky and Vanzir could handle a job as simple as picking up the turkey.

Just then, the door opened and Vanzir burst through. "Where's Delilah?"

"Right here!" Delilah swung around, then stopped. "What the hell?"

I turned to see what the matter was. Vanzir looked frantic. His hair was mussed up and there were what looked like puncture wounds on his forehead. He wiped a string of blood off his cheek.

"What the hell happened to you?" I couldn't take my eyes off him.

"Don't ask! You don't want to know. And Delilah, I advise you to get your ass out of this kitchen before Smoky brings in the turkey." Vanzir looked like he was caught between exasperation and a smirk.

I frowned. "Why on earth would she..." And then—I knew. "No. No. Oh for fuck's sake. Just where did you go to for the turkey?"

Vanzir shrugged. "I wanted to go to The Natural Pantry—you know, where we buy most of the produce that we don't grow. But Smoky had other ideas. Since he's still not entirely thrilled hanging out with me, I decided I wasn't about to make waves."

"And just where did Smoky want to go?"

But Vanzir didn't have time to answer, because in that moment, Smoky strode proudly into the kitchen, with a big mother of a turkey under his arm. Only the turkey? Was still alive. And by alive, I mean, hopping mad. The bird must have weighed a good twenty-five pounds, all right, and it had its tail feathers in an uproar.

He plunked it down on the floor in front of me. "Now, here's a turkey. The ones at the store looked puny so I decided that—"

"What the fuck?" I jumped back as the thing took a stab at the buckles on my boots. "Smoky, have you lost it? We can't cook that thing. The bird is still alive!"

"Not a problem, my love. I'll get up early tomorrow and chop its head off for you and I'll even volunteer to pluck it—"

"What the hell is that?" Iris came back into the room at that moment, and the basket of clean laundry she was carrying went tumbling to the floor. "Just *why* is there a turkey in my kitchen?"

"My kitchen, thank you—you have your own kitchen now, Iris." Hanna glared at Iris, then at Smoky. "But yes, what the hell were you thinking? Get that nasty creature out of here!"

Iris jerked her gaze away from the turkey to stare at Hanna. "Excuse *me*? I may have my own house but this kitchen is still—"

But we were saved from a fight over territory as Delilah shoved her chair back and stumbled to her feet. Fixated on the turkey, a strange, bemused look flickered across her face.

Oh hell, I knew that look! The turkey, meanwhile, was strutting around the room, puffing out his chest, his feather tails were spread wide. Which mean he was getting huffy. And a pissed-off turkey was a pain in the ass.

"Delilah! No—don't!" But I was too late.

Within the blink of any eye, Delilah shifted. One moment my 6'1" sister was standing there. The next moment, a fluffy golden tabby appeared. She promptly went bounding after the bird.

Unimpressed, the turkey lunged at Delilah, narrowly missing her with his beak. Roz tried to grab him from behind and the turkey let out a loud gobble and viciously punched a hole in the incubus's hand.

"Motherfucker!" Roz jerked his hand away. At that moment, Menolly pushed her way around the table. She made a leap for the turkey, but Delilah was in mid-pounce, and the next moment, the two of them collided and went down, Menolly getting an arm full of fur and razor blades. Startled, Delilah tried to claw her way out of Menolly's grasp.

The chaos increased as the kitchen door opened and Nerissa and Chase entered the room. The turkey, seizing his chance, bolted for the open door, throwing Nerissa off guard. She fell against Chase, who caught her, but in doing so, he backed into Hanna, and the tray of biscuits went flying into the fray. The turkey, now caught on the back porch, was hissing and gobbling, stirring for a fight.

"Enough!" I cautiously put down the last of the pies I was holding, trying to make sure it was well away from the edge of the counter. But nobody was listening. So, I did the only thing I could think of. I slipped out into the hall, grabbed my purse, then dashed out the front door and raced around back of the house. The rain and wind were whipping up a storm and by the time I got there, I was soaked through. But, as I yanked open the door to the back porch, the turkey shot through the opening like a bullet out of a gun. I ducked out of his way he raced into the storm. The next thing I knew, Delilah was headed for the door and I slammed it shut before she escaped. A *thunk* on the other side of the door told me she'd hit her head.

Standing there, dripping wet, I listened to the shouts and turmoil coming from within the kitchen. Fuck it. At the very least, we'd need another turkey, preferably one that was dead. Hoisting my purse over my shoulder, I headed for my car.

The turkey let out one last gobble. Turning around, I watched him, an evil gleam in his eye shimmering as he was caught in the light coming from the house.

"You're lucky, sucker. I'd get a move on, if I were you, before you have a dragon, a puma, a panther, and a pissed-off house sprite after you."

As if he understood me, the turkey cocked his head, then turned and ambled into the forest. I jumped in my car and headed to the supermarket. Just another typical D'Artigo Thanksgiving.

A Ghost in the House

This story takes place before Samhain, before Harvest Hunting. It is from Camille's point of view...

"WHAT'S THAT?" I whirled around, once again sure I heard something behind me. But there was nothing there. The past few hours, I'd been sure something was in the house, but the wards showed no intruders, and there didn't seem to be anything out of kilter. Frowning, I glanced over at Menolly and Delilah. We were carving pumpkins for Samhain, and the entire kitchen was a mess of newspapers filled with bright orange guts and seeds.

"I didn't hear anything." Delilah mumbled around a mouthful of Cheetos, her eyes crinkling. "But then again, I was watching the movie."

We'd moved one of the smaller TVs into the

kitchen and were watching Gary Oldman-as-Dracula entice Winona Ryder into a clandestine affair. Even Menolly had to admit, he had his charm, though we all knew Dracula wasn't *really* like that. While we'd never met the vamp personally, the scuttlebutt had it that he was an egomaniacal bloodsucker with a narcissus complex. There was a reason he gave vampires a bad reputation.

"I never understood the appeal." Menolly stabbed one of the pumpkins and began sawing away at the top.

"What about Roman?" I asked, repressing a smile.

"Dracula is no Roman, believe me." But she laughed, and then hopped off the counter. "I'll be right back. I'm going to call Nerissa to find out when she's coming home."

"Camille, can you hand me the Sharpies?" Delilah was drawing on one of the gourds, and doing a pretty good job of it. Maggie was sitting beside her, happy as a clam, scribbling away with a fat pencil on a piece of paper.

I reached for the bag of pens and stopped as something brushed past my hand. *What the...?* The touch was soft, but definitely there. And there was something familiar about it. At first I thought it might be Misty, my ghost kitty, but she was off in the living room, playing with Roz, chasing the red dot toy we'd bought for Delilah.

Maggie let out a *mooph* as Delilah picked her up and moved her to the side. Hanna opened the oven door, and Delilah hurried over to help her extract a batch of cookies from the oven. Peanut butter, chocolate chip, by the smell

"Don't you let me see you with a face full of molten chocolate, Delilah!" Hanna might be strong, but Delilah's desire for hot cookies won out as she grabbed one, darting around Hanna to get it. Hanna let loose with a stern scolding in her native dialect, and I returned my focus to the pumpkin I was carving.

I was doing my best to design a dragon but regardless of all my efforts, the damned thing was looking more like a bedraggled bat. My talent with the carving tool wasn't much better than my talent for punching bad guys.

A few minutes later, Menolly returned, frowning. "Well, fuck. Nerissa has to work late. I wish she could get home before it gets too dark, but that's not going to happen." She paused, looking around. "Where's Maggie?"

I sat up. "Delilah has her—Kitten, where's Maggie?"

Delilah pursed her lips. "I put her on the ground by the table. Isn't she still there?"

I glanced under the table to Delilah's side, but there was no Maggie. "No. Where is she?"

Of course, we immediately went into panic mode. Maggie couldn't have gone far, and the kitchen door was closed, but...

"The front door! Is it open?"

Maggie was learning how to open doors and drawers, and we were watching her all the time now because she was thoroughly into that inquisitive toddler stage. She'd be stuck there for some time. Gargoyles grew very slowly so we had probably a good decade before she grew out of it. And decades after that before she remotely reached puberty.

I hurried to the front door, but it was still locked.

"She couldn't have gotten out through here. I'll check the living room!" As I headed for the living room, Delilah shrieked. Running full tilt into the kitchen, I found her staring at the floor. Maggie's favorite stuffed bear was lying there.

"What's wrong? Why did you scream?"

"The bear! I swear, I saw it floating in the air." She stared at it, eyes wide. "I *know* I saw it—it dropped right as you came in."

"Did you see it, Menolly? Hanna?" I turned to them. Both shook their heads.

"I was checking the bathroom to see if Miss Maggie was there." Hanna walked over to the bear and picked it up. "This was on the table with her last I saw." She headed toward the back of the house. "I'll just check my room." Maggie slept there with her at night, in her crib.

"Nothing out on the back porch." Menolly cocked her head. "I don't know what to think."

"Come quickly!" Hanna's voice echoed from her bedroom and we raced to join her.

There, in the crib, lay Maggie, fast asleep. A faint shimmer sparkled near the bed, and as we watched, the bear floated out of Hanna's hand, through the air.

"Who...what...?" Delilah took a tentative step forward, then hesitated.

I pushed past her and cautiously made my way

over to the crib, the others following me. I stopped right before reaching the sparkling lights.

"Who are you? What do you want with Maggie?" I was ready to go toe-to-toe with any ghost who might be seeking to harm our little girl. But then, Menolly gasped. I turned to see her pointing at the crib, a spark of recognition on her face. Delilah and Hanna were wide-eyed too.

"Look. Camille...look." Delilah's voice was hushed.

I slowly turned back around. There, leaning over Maggie's crib, stood a large, doe-eyed gargoyle. She was a woodland gargoyle, with calico fur just like Maggie. A soft, sad light filled her eyes, and her silky fur waved in the astral wind. She gazed at me, as the bear floated down to snuggle beside our girl. It was then that I noticed the resemblance.

"You're Maggie's mother, aren't you?" I wondered if she could hear me. But, as she smiled and nodded, I realized that she was dead.

"We're taking care of her as best as we can." Delilah slowly moved closer.

"We hope you approve." Menolly gave her a guarded smile, and the gargoyle smiled back.

She turned back to the crib, and with a ghostly hand, reached down to stroke Maggie's face. Sound asleep, our little gargoyle softly giggled, and then turned over to hug her bear. Maggie's mama gave us one last look. Mingled with the sadness, we could see relief, and tears of joy.

"You can come visit her any time you want," I said. "You're welcome here, you know."

She raised one hand, nodded again, and began

to fade away. As the light of her aura grew fainter, I thought I could hear her say, "Thank you. Please, take care of my baby."

"We will," I promised. "We will."

First Touch

From Rozurial's point of view, First Touch takes place between Shadow Rising and Haunted Moon...

A CREAKING WOKE him up. He became aware of the noise as he began to reach the very edge of consciousness. Then, as sleep departed, rolling back like a wave, the sound grew louder, penetrating the last fog that separated Rozurial from the waking world.

As he opened his eyes, he had to stop for a moment. For the hundredth time, or perhaps the thousandth—he had to let himself catch up. Had to remember who he was and how he had become the man he was now.

His dreams often took him home to his childhood, before Dredge destroyed his family. Or they swept him away to the idealistic days of his marriage where Fraale and he lived in love. *Fraale, the only woman who had ever fully won his heart.*

A moment after waking, his heart would slow down, and he'd remember what had taken place during the long centuries of his life. And he'd remember how he'd become an incubus and once again curse Zeus and Hera.

But now, the sound was foremost in his mind. He listened. Whatever it was, it beat a steady cadence, like footsteps falling in an empty hallway.

The studio had been divided into bedrooms— there were four, one of them empty. Roz claimed one, Vanzir another, Shamas the third. Roz's bed was decked out with thick bedclothes, including a heavy comforter that was quilted and inviting. His room was replete with pictures of his adopted family: Camille and Delilah. He wanted a photograph of Menolly, but vamps couldn't take photos. So he'd added one of Iris. Dear Iris, who he had a mad crush on, but knew he could never have.

As the sound echoed again, this time from the common room, Rozurial slid from beneath the comforter, softly edging toward his duster which he kept near the bed. Everyone joked about his arsenal, but he knew they appreciated the weaponry when the shit hit the fan. And truth was, he only felt comfortable when he was armed to the teeth. He'd been a mercenary and bounty hunter far too long to ever feel comfortable unarmed.

A moment later, he slid into the duster, covering his boxers, and tiptoed toward the door. All the time, the noise continued, the low fall of steps, pacing evenly, never varying.

It could be Vanzir, or Shamas, of course, but in his heart he knew it wasn't. There was something out there, all right. Someone—*or some thing*. With all they had been facing lately, with all the ghosts they'd fought, Roz wouldn't have been surprised to find one hitching a ride home.

He leaned against the wall next to the door, his hand on the handle. Then, taking a deep breath, he yanked it open, leaping out into the living room, long dagger ready.

There, pacing the floor, was Hanna, and the front door of the studio was wide open. The woman was from the Northlands, she was sturdy and strong, pretty in a plain way, with the clearest eyes he'd ever seen. But right now, she appeared unaware of him, her face a mask of fear. Roz lowered his blade, then slipped off his duster. She was sleepwalking, so he took care to be as silent as he could as he padded softly to her side.

Hanna didn't wake. She paced blindly, murmuring something beneath her breath. After a moment, Roz was able to make out what she was saying.

"Kjell, can you forgive me? Please, forgive me, my son. Please, understand why I did what I did." Her voice cracked, full of tears, but the look on her face said it all: strained and lost, in search of something to quell her guilt.

Rozurial knew what had happened. Camille had told them, once she was capable of talking about her ordeal. She'd told them how Hanna had helped her escape Hyto's evil lair. How Hanna had tended to her wounds, had helped Camille cope with the aftermath in the wake of the torture sessions the crazed dragon had put her through. And finally, Camille had told them how Hanna had saved her own son by ending his life. There had been no other choice, but everybody knew she carried the stone of that memory around her neck.

And now, apparently, guilt and regret were driving Hanna out of her bed, into a waking dream.

Roz encircled her shoulders with his arm, and led her into his room. She quieted at his touch, and as he tucked her into his bed, she let out a soft sigh and fell into a deep sleep.

That night, Rozurial sat by her side, holding her hand as she slept. He could feel her need. She was lonely. She'd lost her husband, her children, and her home. She'd followed her conscience and it landed her in an alien land, far from where she started. As he reached out to brush a stray hair from her forehead, it occurred to him that they had a great deal in common. They had both lost everything and everyone they loved, and both of them carried memories of the torture and death of their families.

At that moment, Hanna opened her eyes and pulled back, startled. But as her gaze fell on his, Roz leaned down to gently press his lips to hers. Hanna hesitated a moment, then she opened her arms, and welcomed him in.

A Crackle of Flames

This scene—from Delilah's point of view—takes place shortly before Autumn Whispers...

SHADE HAD KINDLED the bonfire in the fire pit and now we sat around the flames, watching them crackle and pop as they spit their way up the wood. The night was cool and leaves were deserting the trees, caught up in the whirl of the wind. It was clear for once, and stars littered the sky overhead, sparkling in the chill of the mid-October evening.

I fiddled with the ring on my finger, the smoky quartz hadn't come off since I'd first accepted it and now it was like a part of me—it was a part of my nature and bound me to Shade in ways I still didn't understand.

He handed me a stick and the bag of marshmallows, and I impaled four of them, then held the candy over the flames, catching the sugar alight. I watched the marshmallows char and bubble up, and then pulled my bounty back, blowing out the flames. I always bit into them too fast, always ended up burning my mouth, and this time I told myself I'd wait. But the scent was too tempting and, once again, I had a mouthful of molten sugar and fanned my tongue.

Shade laughed. "You never learn, do you, Delilah? But his eyes were warm and I knew he was teasing me. He seldom called me sweetie, or love, or honey—almost always my name, though he did call me Kitten like the others. Or when he was in the mood for sex, he'd call me Pussycat.

I shrugged. "What can I say? I like to live dangerously." I took another bite, but the candy had cooled enough and this time, I happily finished it off.

We were down by Birchwater Pond, where we'd installed picnic tables and the fire pit and a covered shelter. Tonight, Shade and I had felt the need for some privacy, other than in our rooms, so we'd decided to spend the evening here, under the shadow of the night.

This was our time. Autumn, the season of our master, The Autumn Lord. Hi'ran was strong with us tonight, looming like a great shadow of fire and smoke. I could feel him in the trees, in the flames, in the very air with its chill tang that bit into the skin ever so slightly.

"He's here." I glanced at Shade.

"I know. He's watching us. He's watching the world. There's something afoot and the Harvestmen are alert."

"Samhain is coming—perhaps that has something to do with it?" The season of death was upon us, the season of the Witch, the season of the cauldron. Camille's season, with her death magic. Menolly's season—the time of the vampire. And now...now that I was a Death Maiden, my season, too. We lived in a world of darkness and flame, but it was comforting as well as melancholy.

Shade closed his eyes, leaning back to listen to the wind. After a few minutes he shook his head. "This is not in the natural order of things. I sense something approaching." He scooted closer to me and draped his arm around my shoulders. His skin, the color of a strong latte, blended into the night, and his honey-amber hair gleamed under the pale starlight.

I reached out, placed my lips against his, and gently kissed him. Then, he was holding me close, pulling me into his embrace, his mouth fastened against mine. I slid off the bench onto the ground, pulling him down with me, and there, against the wet grass, in the light of the flames, I pulled off my jacket and shirt, as he tugged against the snaps on my jeans.

Struggling out of them, I slid astride him. He had shoved his jeans down, and now his cock was erect. I lowered myself onto him, hungry. I needed his touch, needed his thrust. I moaned as he took hold of my waist, guiding me as I rode him in the dark of the night. And then, Hi'ran was there, with us, staring up at me from Shade's eyes.

I could feel my master, feel him through my

lover, and the swell of his energy rose up to embrace me like a warm shroud, encasing me in the shadows of death and repose, that solemn embrace that welcomes everyone at the end of their life. I cried out as Shade's fingers raced over my body—burning brightly. The sparks set of my desire, and I cried out, wanting it harder, faster, deeper.

Hi'ran laughed, his voice echoing through Shade's, and I answered the call—riding him now, my wild dragon, my shadow walker who had come through worlds to walk by my side. I loved him, fiercely, like the predator I was.

Panther snarled, reveling in our passion, and as I came close to the edge, Shade rolled me over, thrusting deeply from behind, driving himself home into my pussy as his balls thudded against my ass. And then, a wild shriek pierced the night and I realized the shriek had come from me—my voice echoing as it hung in the air before the wind snatched it away. I let go as Shade gave one final thrust, and we were swept up into the night, fueled by the fires of Hi'ran.

As the ripples of orgasm slowly left my body, a stark fear hit me. Something was headed our way, and this might be the last time we'd be able to let go of control before we had to face the oncoming danger.

Dreaming Death

Another short scene taking place shortly before Autumn Whispers, between Delilah and her sister Arial...

I KNEW I was wandering in my dreams. The more I trained at Haseofon, the more I seemed to blur the lines between dreaming and waking during the sleep state. Greta hadn't summoned me, for once, but still, there stood the temple—huge and beautiful and stately. I looked up at it with pride in my heart. I'd come to love my calling, to take pride in the fact that I was the Autumn Lord's only living Death Maiden.

Slowly climbing the steps, I examined my feelings. A knot of dread filled the pit of my stomach. I knew I hadn't made any mistakes, but there was something wrong—I could feel it to my core. I prayed it wasn't anything I'd have to get embroiled in—my sisters and I had enough on our plates right now.

As I entered the temple, everything seemed normal. Maybe the stress of life had been getting to me. Maybe it was really just my imagination. The other Death Maidens seemed to be going about their normal business—training, talking, reading, making music...everything looked perfectly fine on the surface.

A noise to my right startled me. I turned to find Arial standing there.

My twin sister who had died at birth, Arial looked like me except that her hair was waist length and sable brown, and when she was in her Were form, she was a leopard. Only here in Haseofon, the temple of the Death Maidens, could she appear in her two-legged form. Whenever she left, she had to wander the realms as a spirit leopard.

But now, she threw her arms around my neck. "Sister! I hoped you would come. I need to talk to you."

While she was smiling, her brow crinkled with worry, and her voice was guarded. She pulled me back into the private chamber in which she made her home. It was done up in rich browns and rusts, in aubergine and sage. The bed was huge and I sank into the mattress, wanting nothing more than to turn into my Tabby self and go to sleep.

But Arial joined me on the bed, cross-legged, leaning forward. "I've had a dream. A bad one. I need to tell you about it."

I frowned. "A nightmare? What was it?" It seemed odd—sitting here with my dead sister discussing bad dreams, but let's face it. My world was made of odd and not likely to calm down any time soon.

She played with the hem of her gown. Arial liked to dress in floaty gauze skirts and peasant blouses. She wore flowers in her hair, too. She would have made the perfect Bohemian back Earthside, even though she would have been a few decades out of date.

"I dreamed of fire and smoke. Of buildings crashing to the ground. I dreamed of people screaming, trying to escape the lightning. I dreamed a powerful death. And another, and yet another. And ten thousand more atop that." Arial looked over at me, but I had the feeling she wasn't seeing me. Instead, she was looking through me, into a vision where I could not follow her.

"Do you know where? When? Who?" My voice was a whisper.

I knew better than ignore her warnings. Nobody in Haseofon dreamed just for fun. Whether visions of the future or from the past, all of the Death Maidens who lived here dreamed of realities spinning out on the web. Or of events that had a good chance of coming to pass. Because she lived with them, my sister dreamed the same way.

She paused, as if listening to a voice inside her head, then frowned.

"The spirits won't tell me. But be careful. You and Camille and Menolly. Death is coming, and not with easy grace. Death is coming in on the wings of flame and storm and fury. And you will be in the thick of it. Walk softly, sister. I do not want to see any of you cross the veil." Pausing, Arial seemed to be deciding whether or not to say something else, but then she just smiled softly. "That is all I'm allowed to say."

Burning with curiosity, I wanted to ask her more, but I knew it would be useless. So we talked of other things, and finally, late into the night I kissed her and prepared to return to my body.

As I left her door she called softly, "You won't remember this, when you wake. But...some part of you will be aware, and your reactions will be swifter than they might. Maybe it will help you through the coming days."

I nodded, hoping she was wrong, though those living in the temple never were. As I hurried home to my body, a raven caught my attention. It screamed loud and long, and I could feel the storm on the horizon. And it was heading directly for us.

Surprises

This takes place about a month before Autumn Whispers, one year after Trillian and Camille's wedding...

"YOU WHAT?" I couldn't believe what I was hearing. Trillian could *not* have said what I thought he just said. But he smiled at me, in that cunning way he had and I knew I'd heard right.

"I'm crossing over to Otherworld for a few days. I leave right now." He slipped his backpack over his shoulder and gave me a horribly perfunctory kiss, then dodged out the back door before I could say another word.

My temper at a low boil, I clenched my fists and whirled around as Kitten tapped me on the shoulder.

"You okay?"

My expression must have screamed *No, I'm NOT okay* because she grimaced and took a step back, holding up her hands. "Whatever it was, I didn't do it!"

I exhaled slowly, trying to calm down. "I know, I know. I'm just furious at Trillian right now."

I wanted to kick something, or maybe throw something like his new Waterford clock he'd bought that I didn't really even like. But throwing things? So not my style.

Instead, I settled for yanking the garbage out from under the sink and stomping out the kitchen door to pile it in the bin. From there, we'd cart it to the dump. Our house in Belles-Faire wasn't on the main trash collection route, so we were responsible for taking care of the trash ourselves.

Delilah was smart enough not to follow me, and I stood in the crisp October air, breathing deeply as I tried to relax and take stock.

I couldn't believe that Trillian had taken off. *Not today.*

Fucking men. He knows what today is, and he knows that I expect something more than an "I'll see you."

Sometimes I wondered why I'd gotten married at all. To any of my husbands, for that matter. Right now, all three of my men had been acting inconsiderate. It crossed my mind, maybe I should just pack up and take a few days for myself. Go home to Otherworld and hang out by the shores of Lake Y'Leveshan. I could set up camp, kick back, read a few books, go visit the High Priestess De-risa, in the Grove of the Moon Mother. Hell, for that matter, I could stop in and see Aunt Rythwar. In general, maybe I really needed a breather from the constant stress we were under.

The sun glimmered through afternoon clouds as I strolled over to the herb garden. The garden was starting to look a little raggedy around the edges. We'd moved the kitchen herbs to the greenhouse that the men had built as an add-on to Iris's cottage, but I'd kept my magical herbs here. They needed to stay in the magical circle in which I'd planted them, at least until they were harvested. I knelt down by the mandrake and whispered a hello to it. A few drops of rain from the high clouds made me glance up at the sky. We'd be in the thick of storm weather soon. It was almost time to compost around the base of all the perennials so that when the rainy season did hit, they'd be safe from the chill. Because the first frost wouldn't be far behind.

A little bit calmer, my thoughts returned to Trillian and his abrupt departure. How could he? But if I dwelled on it, I'd just get upset again, so I pushed it out of my mind and decided a walk would do me good. I'd head down to Birchwater Pond. The water always soothed me. But as I set foot on the path, Delilah called to me from the back porch. She sounded insistent, and so—with a sigh—I glanced one last time over my shoulder at the path before heading back inside.

"Since Trillian's gone tonight, I thought you might like to start planning out what we need to do before the rainy season hits. House stuff—you know? What needs to be fixed, what needs replaced, all that." Kitten thrust the household notebook into my arms. "With Iris so near to having her twins, I figured that you would probably want to take over. Hanna doesn't know enough about running the place yet, and she can't read English."

Lovely. *Just* what I wanted to do today. Grumbling under my breath, I sat down at the kitchen table. "Well, bring me a plate of cookies and a latte, then." I glared up at her. "And speaking of... where is Hanna?"

"I gave her the afternoon off. She wanted to do some shopping." Delilah made me a quad-shot iced caramel latte, and set a plate of Hanna's peanut butter cookies on the table next to me. She settled in next to me, and we began to run over the upkeep schedule on the house. After about thirty minutes, we were knee deep in plans, and there was no good place to stop, so I decided to write off the day and throw myself into getting the task finished.

The afternoon wore away before I knew it, and I didn't look up until Hanna bustled in from wherever she'd been. She wasn't carrying any bags, so I assumed they were still in the car, and that Vanzir must have driven her to the mall. I glanced at the clock. Almost six, and my stomach was rumbling.

"I guess we might as well order a pizza or something." I stood, wincing as I realized I'd been sitting for three hours straight.

Delilah shrugged. "I'm not that hungry."

I looked at her strangely. *Kitten was turning down pizza?* That was a new one. A moment later, she swore under her breath.

"What's wrong?"

"I left my dagger down by the pond when I was

there last. I can't believe I did that." She frowned.

"Well, go get it." By now, I was ready to pack it in for the day and just go upstairs with a bag of chips, lock my door, and tell Smoky and Morio they could sleep in the parlor.

"Camille, pretty please, won't you go do it for me? I've got a stomachache and was about to go lie down." Delilah turned on her sad-kitty face.

I groaned. "*Really? Really?* Oh for fuck's sake… it's always *Camille to the rescue*, isn't it?"

With a sigh, I slammed through the back door and headed out into the backyard, ready to blow. I stomped across the yard to the path that led to Birchwater Pond. Lovely, just lovely. I was always the fall-back person. Don't feel like doing something? *Just ask Camille.* It had been this way all my life and I was sick and tired of it.

As I passed the place where Hyto had captured me, I shuddered, unwelcome memories flooding over me. But Smoky and the men had cut down the trees his father had blasted, and in their place, they'd planted rose bushes that bloomed well into the autumn, trying to replace bad memories with prettier ones. It had been Trillian's idea. Right now, that didn't make me feel any better. But their spicy scent spiraled down to catch my attention. I couldn't help but pause and close my eyes.

As evening breeze flickered past, I listened to the echo of birdsong and caught another deep breath, letting it out slowly before I opened my eyes and continued on. Maybe this wasn't so bad after all. I'd wanted to go down to the pond earlier, and Delilah's forgetfulness *had* gotten me out of the house. I'd apologize to Kitten when I got back. After all, if she was really sick, then there was no harm in helping her.

I slowed my pace, letting the approaching dusk wash over me. By the time I came to the opening leading out to the shores around Birchwater Pond, I was calm again. But wait...there were lights flickering from the grotto. There shouldn't be—not this time of year. Yes, we'd built picnic tables and benches and a shelter near the pond so we could come down here in inclement weather for our rituals and holidays, but there shouldn't be anybody there right now.

I cautiously slid to the side of the trail, easing toward the lights. Could they be eye catchers? But we didn't have eye catchers Earthside. What about will-o'-the-wisps? Maybe we had another invasion of the freaking pests? They could range from mischievous to highly dangerous.

Just as I was about ready to return to the house for backup, I heard music. One of my favorite softer bands—Tamaryn. Now, will-o'-the-wisps wouldn't be trying to lure me in with an MP3 player!

Frowning, wondering what was going on, I stepped into the clearing to get a better view.

"Surprise!"

The onslaught of laughter startled me as the majority of our household jumped out from behind bushes. Morio and Smoky were first, then Shade, Nerissa, Roz and Vanzir. Behind me, Delilah and Hanna laughingly raced in from off the path behind me, carrying Maggie.

"Menolly will be here when she wakes up," Kitten said.

"What is this?" I now noticed that the picnic tables were covered with food, the lights were Christmas lights strung from tree to tree, and the music was coming from the sound system we'd wired through the woods. There were also presents on one of the picnic tables, wrapped in pretty paper.

"Happy anniversary, love." Trillian stepped out from behind a cedar tree. "You didn't *really* think I'd forget, did you? You honestly believed I'd run off to Otherworld on our anniversary if I didn't have to?" He was laughing, and he opened his arms.

I stared at him, briefly wanting to kill him for what he'd put me through. Then, with a laugh, letting the day slide into the past, I moved into his arms, and pressed my lips against his.

Meetings

Here's a short scene that gives you just a glimpse of the first time that Maria, the D'Artigo Sisters' mother, met Sephreh ob Tanu...

THE FIRST TIME they met, it was shortly after summer solstice, in a little outdoor café off a back alley. Maria had been there many times, always alone, to eat lunch while she sketched. Pastries were expensive. Due to the war, sugar was rare, and they were chewy, made from whole grains rather than white flour. But they tasted good, and were big enough to make lunch from, along with a piece of cheese and a glass of wine.

She wasn't wealthy, but the inheritance from her foster parents had left her with enough money to go abroad, to study art. And—though she never admitted it to any of her friends—she had come to Spain to look for family she had never met. Family only rumored to still exist. The journey had been dangerous and her friends thought she was crazy. Coming into a country so soon after civil war had ended, with yet another war waging not so far away in Europe—no, it didn't really make for san ity. But so far, she'd been lucky.

Maria had ignored all the warnings. She'd always gone her own way. After all, nothing waited for her at home. Her foster parents were dead. She had no boyfriends nor close friends to tie her down. And perhaps the most important factor: She had no clue about what she wanted to do in life. All she knew was that she was searching for something, and she wouldn't find it at home. So she'd packed her bags and come to Spain, and even though she didn't really know anybody over here, she loved the city and the culture, and the old world charm.

And that was how she'd ended up here: In a small village, on holiday from the university, drinking red wine, while she contemplated the rest of her life.

A moment later, the hairs on the back of her neck stood up. She stiffened, uncertain what had alarmed her. As she looked around, trying to figure out what it was that suddenly had her uneasy, she couldn't see anything out of the ordinary. There were no militarists in sight. No sounds of bombers or explosions—frequent visitors over the past couple of years. No, nothing seemed out of the ordinary.

"May I sit with you?"

The voice was deep, smooth and wary. But

it struck a chord inside of her. Even before she looked to see to who was speaking, Maria knew she wanted to hear more. She slowly raised her gaze.

The man standing in front of her was slightly above average height—maybe near to six feet, maybe a hair under. He was obviously European, for he had jet black wavy hair that reached his lower shoulder blades, and eyes the color of...

Maria blinked. For a moment, she could have sworn his eyes were violet, but that was impossible. *I must be tired*, she thought, rubbing her hand across her face. She looked again. This time, his eyes seemed pale blue, impossibly frosty but still...

"Please, join me." She wasn't in the habit of inviting strange men to sit with her, but there was something about him that resonated inside her. She realized she wanted to know his name.

As he sat, she realized how pale he was against the black suit. He looked almost albino, with creamy skin that would be the envy of every woman around. As she curled a tendril of hair around her finger, she realized that her heart was beating faster and thoughts she tended to keep under lock and key were rising, along with a heat between her thighs.

"What might be your name?" Again, the deep, smooth voice glided over the words, sending a ripple of hunger through her body. She couldn't place the accent, but it was lilting and sensuous.

She ducked her head. "Maria D'Artigo. I'm from the United States."

"Hello, Maria D'Artigo," the man said, a smile playing over his lips. "My name is Sephreh ob

Tanu. Can I buy you another glass of wine?" And then, he leaned forward, his hand gently brushing hers, and in that single moment, she fell, hard into a dangerous stream of thought.

"My life has just changed forever," she thought. A door had just opened, and no matter where it led, she was going to follow. With a winsome grin, she tossed her blonde hair over her shoulders, and walked out of her past, into her future.

Part Two

Men of Otherworld: Collection One

The Hunger

I've often thought about Rozurial's life when he was with Fraale, and that fateful day when Zeus and Hera forever changed their lives. This is that story.

THE WILD ROSES were blooming in the garden, which meant that soon it would be time to gather the honey and start harvesting apples. Rozurial loved this time of year when everything was still warm and golden, but the autumn called from just over the hill. As the sun crept over the horizon, streaking the early dawn with golden tongues of fire, Roz sat on a slope near his home, chewing on a piece of grass, as he contemplated what needed doing before nightfall.

Fraale, his wife—the love of his life and the one constant in his world—was baking bread in the outdoor oven. It was still too warm to heat up the house, so she had been doing all the summer cooking outdoors. She had shooed him out when he stopped to grab a roll and some meat for breakfast, laughing and cussing out the loose bricks that were making the cooking precarious.

Now, stomach full for the morning, Roz stretched back, hands under his head, and ticked off a mental list of chores that lie ahead of him. Milk the goats, harvest vegetables to dry out under the sun for winter. The berries were ripe and Fraale wanted to get to her jam-making soon. He also needed to mend the fence in the southern pasture before the goats broke it down and ran amok.

With a sigh, he pushed himself to his feet. The sooner he got busy, the sooner he'd get done. As he stood there, the morning light glinting off his waist-length hair that coiled down his back, a shadow cast cross him from a nearby tree. A sudden chill raced up his spine and he let out low growl, dropping into a crouch, squatting as he scanned the horizon for any sign of movement. But the only signs of life were the insects and birds that filled the meadow, and the raggle-taggle herd of goats that had followed him up from the lower pastures. Frowning, he eased himself back to his feet.

"It can't be him," Roz whispered. "It can't be Dredge. Not in daylight. Not at sunrise."

The last time he'd felt this same, sudden fear, he'd still been on the hunt and his instincts had been keen. At times, Rozurial feared that life with Fraale had blunted them—that withdrawing from the relentless pursuit of the vampire who had killed his entire family had been a mistake. But most of the time now, he was happy. And when the memories swept down to fill his nightmares, Fraale was there to wake him up.

He scanned the horizon again. *Nothing*.

Roz exhaled slowly, breathing out the fear. Fear was dangerous. Fear was more dangerous than the adversary you were afraid of. Fear could kill.

When his pulse had stopped racing, he closed his eyes and listened. There were no silences in the bird song, there was no sudden cessation of insects thrumming. The wind felt the same—no sudden shifts, no scents other than what should be there. Finally, he let it go. Opening his eyes, he glanced down as one of the goats ran over to nuzzle his side. He patted her head. Trika stared up at him, then followed him as he started down off the slope.

"You'd think by now I could let the past go. Sometimes the monsters of the world make our memories into even worse creatures. Sometimes, their worst attack is to make our entire lives a living nightmare of fear."

Trika let out a bleat, as if answering him.

"You bugger, you. Go on with you, get to the herd and fill your belly." He shooed her off, laughing.

Dredge couldn't be here. Vampires slept in daylight, even the strongest and the baddest of them. And Dredge wasn't the hunter, not this time. No, Dredge wouldn't know him from a rock. Because Dredge was halfway to insane, and the only thing that mattered to him was the current kill, the current prey. Rozurial had hunting him across the world and back again before giving up to settle in and have as normal of a life as he could. Last he heard, Dredge was tracking through Ceredream, feeding off the whores and the homeless—castaways who wouldn't be missed. No, it wasn't Dredge that had set him on alert. Just *who* it was, he didn't know. But not Dredge.

STOPPING IN AT the house to pick up his lunch bucket and to give Fraale a kiss, Rozurial found her cussing out the summer oven. She had burned two loaves of bread thanks to the uneven heating and now she swung around, hands on hips.

"You promised me you'd repair this. I can't do the harvest preserves until you fix it." She was pretty—plump and round, with brown hair and eyes that flashed when she was angry...and when she wanted to make love.

Roz swept her into his arms, his lips pressing against hers. She was warm and soft, cushioned in all the right places, and as he buried his nose in her hair, all he wanted to do was sweep her into the bedroom and kiss his way down her body. But she pushed her way out of his embrace after a sound kiss.

"Chores first. The fields will not till themselves, and the fruits won't fall into the baskets on their own accord. Now, when are you going to fix my oven?" But her eyes danced as she slapped him on the chest.

He grinned. "Tonight. I promise you, I'll fix both

the summer oven and the fireplace. Now, give me my lunch, woman, and make me some cookies today? Please?" Again, the boyish smile flashed as he gently smacked her on the ass. Even if settling down had dulled his senses, it was worth it—the sun on her hair, the smells of home around him. The sense of family he'd lost thanks to Dredge in childhood, he'd gained when he met Fraale.

She pushed a bucket into his hands. "There's bread and cheese, meat and cake, and a bottle of milk. Go on with you, then."

And so, Rozurial headed off to build and mend and harvest and generally take care of business.

HE WAS PARTWAY through the afternoon when he got the feeling something was wrong. The same shiver he'd felt in the morning hit him, and he shaded his eyes. From the pasture he was standing in, the house was barely visible—a faint protrusion on the horizon. He was a twenty minute walk from home, on the highest hill of their property, staring through the fields of corn and root vegetables. Trying to shake the feeling, he went back to shoring up the last boundary marker that was leaning precariously, then—unable to shake the worry—decided to head back home early.

On his way, his walk became a jog became an outright run. Roz was in good shape, and by the time he saw the fence that divided their house from the gardens, he slowed, hoping he wasn't making a fool of himself. Fraale would probably laugh herself silly at his expense—there were no signs of fire, no signs of trouble. He debated whether to just turn back and go finish bringing in the wagon filled with berries and fruit, and carrots and corn that he'd picked during the afternoon, but a noise made him pause.

Slowly, he edged around to the side of the house. There, tied to the gate, was a white stallion—huge and gleaming in the late afternoon sun. No saddle...so whoever owned it must have either been leading it by the bridle, or riding bareback.

A sudden scream from inside the house broke through his thoughts and he whirled, racing toward the door. As he burst into the parlor, the first thing he saw was a Fraale, trying to get out of the clutches of a tall, white haired man who was attempting to kiss her. Roz leaped forward, grabbing hold of the man's arm to pull him off his wife.

With one shrug, the man tossed him aside like he was a limp rag. Roz shook his head, sitting up dazed. What the hell? He was strong—the man looked older, how could he have...and then he noticed what the man was wearing. A white cloak, over a white and gold gown belted by a golden sash. A faint bluish glow surrounded him, and when he turned to look at Rozurial, his eyes were the glow of early morning sky.

"*Zeus*..." Roz slowly stood up. "Zeus?" he whispered again.

The god let out a grumbling sigh and, taking his hands off Fraale, turned to Rozurial and crossed his arms. "Doesn't anyone ever kneel anymore?"

Roz's eyes narrowed. When he was very young, he had hidden away, watching his family forced to kneel at the feet of a monster. He had never been on his knees in front of anyone since that day, and he didn't plan to start now.

"Leave my wife alone. Leave my house."

Zeus glanced at Fraale, who was adjusting her dress. She backed away, skirting towards Roz, the expression on her face one of mingled terror and disbelief.

"Fine way of showing hospitality to a wandering stranger." Zeus's words were mildly slurred and the scent of wine filled the air as he hiccupped.

Great. Not only a lecherous god, but a drunken lecherous god. Roz knew better than attack him again—he no longer had the element of surprise, and the truth was, now that he realized it was Zeus before him, he was scared shitless. Gods didn't play by mortal rules and while they could be killed, it would take someone far stronger than Rozurial to manage it. Not to mention the fact that, should he manage to hurt the god, the rest of the Olympians would be on his ass and he'd be toast.

Fraale was almost to Roz's side when a whirl of wind swept through the door and a woman suddenly stood at the entrance, glaring at Zeus. She too, wore white robes and gold adornments, and her hair was coiled on her head in golden ringlets. Her eyes narrowed, she glanced from Zeus to Fraale, then back again to Zeus.

"I knew it. I knew you were gallivanting again. And what do I find? You slumming with the dregs of the Fae. You can't even keep yourself to our station—the nymphs would be better than this! Look at her—she's not even pretty."

Hera. It had to be Hera. Which meant they could be in one hell of a lot of trouble. Zeus was bad enough but the two had a marriage made in hell, and rumor had it that getting between them when they were arguing was tantamount to a death sentence.

Roz slowly reached out for Fraale's hand and, once it was secure in his, began edging his way way toward the door, slow step by slow step. If they could make it outside, they might be able to run and hide until the divine couple patched things up and left. At worst, Roz thought, they could leave town and start over somewhere else.

His plan might have worked—they almost had managed to reach the door—when Hera spun around, breaking off from browbeating Zeus, who was listening to her with an *Oh, fuck, here we go again* look on his face.

"Where do you think you're going?" Hera was suddenly in front of them, moving in a blur of speed. "I did not give you permission to leave my presence." Her eyes were steely blue, and Roz's stomach lurched at the wave of anger rolling off the goddess. It raced like a tidal wave, surrounding both him and Fraale, forcing them to their knees. Roz struggled against the pressure, but found himself unable to move or speak.

Fraale let out a whimper as Hera stepped closer and reached out to cup her chin. "So, you are the girl who captured my husband's attention this time, are you?" Her voice had become very soft, which was more frightening than when she was screaming.

Roz struggled, still holding Fraale's hand. She squeezed tightly, and he could feel her fear through their contact. He desperately wanted to break free, to drag her outside away from all of this, but his body refused to obey.

Hera leaned down, staring into Fraale's eyes. "You wish to seduce the husbands of other women so badly? Then I'll make it easier for you."

Fraale whimpered again, and managed to eke out a whisper. "No...I did not...I didn't touch him—I didn't ask..."

"Oh, none of you touch him. None of you ask for his attentions. I've heard it so many times I might as well commission a sad song for you. But still, I find him in your house, and his scent is on you." Hera's eyes flashed with a dangerous light. "His hands were on you."

"Leave the girl alone." Zeus seemed to break out of his stupor and strode forward. "We've been through this before. You know my eye wanders... you knew this when you agreed to marry me."

"Your eye may wander, but your hands and body follow and therein lies the problem, my husband." Hera shook her head, a painful look crossing her face. "How many times have you apologized and then I find this...again and again. *I will not stand for it*. I will not stand by and watch you cavort with some mortal trollop." She turned abruptly, slapping him across the face. "I ask for so little—I ask for respect and for honor. If you're going to take lovers, at least take them from those worthy of the attentions of a god. Not some...some...succubus."

"Hera, you are my wife and the mother of the gods—compose yourself!" Zeus blustered up, and a roll of thunder split the air outside. Through the window, Rozurial could see one hell of a bank of storm clouds coming in as rain began to lash the ground.

But Zeus's order fell on deaf ears. Hera sputtered, then, glancing back at Fraale, she let out a snort. "I said trollop. You want to seduce husbands away from their wives? Then do it right, at least." And with that, she reached out and brushed her hand across Fraale's forehead, then in a flash of light, vanished, laughing.

Fraale let go of Rozurial's hand, screaming as she dropped to the ground. Roz tried to go to her, but Zeus reached out, held him back.

"Do not touch her, boy. Not yet." The god stared at him, his voice a whisper. Roz tried to break free but Zeus held him steady.

Fraale was convulsing on the ground, frothing at the mouth as her eyes rolled back in her head. She let out one long, piercing scream as Roz began to weep. He was losing her—he knew it. She was dying and he couldn't even comfort her.

But instead of collapsing, the fit began to pass, and Fraale lie there, her eyes closed, but he could tell she was breathing—almost panting. Zeus let go of him then, and stood watching as Roz fell to his knees beside his love.

He felt for her pulse, which was rapid but steady, and then brushed her hair back away from her face. There seemed to be something different about her—she was the same and yet...there was something that had changed. As she slowly opened her eyes, the glint in them made him nervous.

"Love, love are you all right?" Roz slid his arm behind her back and helped her sit up. "What happened—" He stopped. The woman in his arms was not his Fraale. Not entirely. Of that much, he was certain.

She let out a long sigh, almost exasperated. And then, without a word, she drew him in for a kiss, her tongue playing against his. She was warm in his arms, pliable, and he found himself wanting to fuck her right there, in front of Zeus. All he could think about was how beautiful this woman of his was, and how she needed him. But then, as the kiss went on, he began to feel dizzy and with a start, realized that he was losing consciousness. Another moment, and the world went black.

"YOU AWAKEN, THEN?" Zeus was sitting there at the table, staring at him.

Roz realized he was stretched out on the length of polished wood, his head aching and feeling like he'd been sick for a long, long time. He tried to sit up, but Zeus shook his head and pushed him back down.

"Rest yourself. You are still weak."

"What...what happened?" And then, he remembered. "Fraale! Fraale? Where's my wife." He brushed away Zeus's hand and forced himself to a seated position. The room began to spin, but he squinted, staring at one spot on the wall to help him focus enough so that he could manage sitting up.

"Your wife. She drained you. She would have killed you if I hadn't intervened, but truth is: She didn't realize that she was siphoning off so much energy from you. She's hungry, she needs to feed." The god sounded genuinely sorry.

Rozurial frowned, trying to understand what Zeus was saying. Hunger? Siphoning off energy? Oh no...he couldn't mean... "Hera, she turned Fraale into a vampire?" His heart was about to rip out of his chest and shatter on the ground.

Zeus quickly held up a hand. "No, no—rest easy on that. Your wife is no vampire."

"Then what are you talking about?" Thoroughly confused and exhausted, Rozurial turned helplessly toward Zeus. "What happened? Tell me."

Zeus suddenly looked old. Old as the hills, old as time. His shoulders slumped. "Hera turned your wife into a succubus."

And that was all he needed to say. Roz knew what succubi were. Sexually charged energy vampires—minor demons, to be precise. The thought of Fraale, wanton and seeking to feed her hunger, churned in his stomach. He wanted to shout, to rail against the heavens, but it would do no good. The *'heavens'* were sitting in his living room. The *'heavens'* had caused this.

"What am I going to do? I love her—I love her and I can't stand the thought of losing her."

At that moment, the door opened and Fraale

stood there. Her dress was different—she was wearing a lower cut gown that sparkled in the evening light, and her eyes were dewy. Her lips looked so moist that it made him hard, rock-hard and ready to fuck her.

She moved slowly through the room to him. "Rozurial...I love you. I'm so sorry." Her voice was as broken as his heart.

He turned to Zeus. "This is your fault. Fix it. Do whatever you need to but fix it."

Zeus looked from Fraale to Roz, back to Fraale again. "I cannot undo what Hera did—no one but she has the power to undo her magic, and she has a long, harsh memory. But...I will do the only thing I can think of to help." He stood, then reached out and touched Rozurial.

Roz felt something beginning to shift inside, a warm glow that quickly became a raging fire, rampaging through his body—burning the cells, shifting and changing him. As he fell back on the table, his body beginning to spasm, his last thought was, "I'm dying." And then, the darkness hit again.

"SO HERE WE are." Fraale gazed at him, her luminous eyes shimmering with tears.

"Wherever here is." Roz pressed his lips into a thin line as he stared out the window. He was hungry—the ache was always there now. The desire to touch, to kiss, to run his fingers along feminine flesh, to taste the energy that charged him up like a fresh eye catcher, about to explode. No matter how much he and Fraale had come together over the past weeks, the ache and need couldn't be satiated, for either of them. Now, they were facing each other, honestly, the naked truth painfully evident.

"I love you." He swung around, catching her hands in his. "You know how much I love you—I never wanted anything more than to grow old with you, to have children, to make some semblance of a normal life. *You know that*, don't you?"

Her breath was ragged, this time not from desire, but tears. "Don't say it—there has to be a way we can get back to normal. Every man I touch, reminds me that he's not you. But I can't stop—I can't stop myself. I killed someone last night, and that will never happen again, I swear it. If I have to slit my own throat, I'll never kill any man again with my kiss. Can't we try again? Can't we try once more—we can sustain each other—" But her pleas fell away.

Rozurial's own eyes were wet. "We've tried. Every day we make this pledge. Every night...we roam the astral and hunt down victims. We can't do it anymore—this guilt will eat us alive. If we stay together, we'll drive each other mad. I can't stand to think of you with other men but I know you need them. *I know your hunger because I feel it myself.*"

How many times had he blamed Zeus? How many times had he stared at himself in the mirror, seeing the glamour that the god had given him when he changed him into an incubus? How many times had he cursed the gods who had destroyed their house?

Fraale leaned over, sobbing so hard he thought she might break. She fell to her knees, pressing her head on his lap. "Don't leave me. Don't leave... what will I do without you?"

"My love, that's not the question. The question is, what will we do to each other if we stay together? I know it hurts you to see me with other women, too. But...I think we have to accept—there's no going back. The healers and witches told us that. Zeus and Hera ignore our prayers. Face it, Fraale, we're stuck like this."

And that was the kicker—they were stuck. Stuck in a glamorous world of sex and charm and passion...but they couldn't share it with each other without destroying what love they had left.

Fraale pushed herself to a cross legged position and wiped her tears on her sleeve. She gazed up at him, and he saw the resignation in her eyes. "I know," she whispered. "I know this is the end." She let out a shuddering sigh, and then stood. "Rozurial, I will always love you. I'll always miss you. And I'll always hate the gods—with the last of my breath, I will curse them."

He rose, taking her in his arms, pulling her tight against his body. She fit—they fit together, and that was the hellish part. They had come together and built their love and their life, and now, in love, they were having to dissemble everything they had ever known.

"Fraale, you'll always be in my heart. But any chance we have for happiness...it means we have to part. We have to walk away and not look back, because the pain of what we've lost...there's no getting past it otherwise. I look at you and remember what joy we had."

She pressed her cheek on his shoulder. "And I look at you, and I remember the promise of the future. Now, everything is shrouded in fog." Then, resolutely, she took a step back. "Promise me, in a year, we'll return here to see how...to see if...to check on each other? Promise me—on your oath. That way we won't do anything stupid."

He nodded, understanding the unspoken message. "I promise. One year, here, we will meet." He glanced around at the tidy home they had made. "I sold the goats to the farmer across the hill. Your half of the money is on the table."

Fraale shivered. "I don't want to leave. I was so happy here."

"I know." Rozurial picked up the bag of coins and pressed them into her hand. "But you go first... that way...it won't seem so empty when you leave. That way you'll remember me here."

"I will never forget you, my love. Never." Fraale slowly turned and, tears silently streaking down her cheeks, headed for the door. As it swung shut behind her, Rozurial took one more look around the house that had been his home for too short of a time.

He slid into a long duster—the autumn had finally hit—into which he had crammed every weapon he could think of. Placing a hat over his long curls, he inhaled sharply, then let out a long sigh and and headed toward the door, wondering if he would ever see his beloved Fraale again.

Pushing the thought aside, he stepped out into the evening air. Reports put Dredge still in Ceredream. That seemed the most likely place to catch the vampire who had destroyed his childhood. Because if he couldn't kill the monster who had destroyed his marriage, he was damned well going to track down the one who had murdered his parents and siblings. And this time, using the new powers that had come with transforming into an incubus, Rozurial swore he would cross every world necessary to find the vampire and stake him.

Chasing Sharah

The first date is always awkward—and it seemed to me that Chase and Sharah would feel even more uncomfortable, given their circumstances.

IT REALLY DIDN'T feel right. Chase had always been extremely good about keeping his private affairs separated from work and right now, he didn't feel at all comfortable. But one thing had led to another, and now, here he was, standing on Sharah's doorstep with flowers in hand, staring at the doorbell. He shifted, uncertain whether he could actually go through with this, but then he thought about how uncomfortable work would be tomorrow if he stood up the elfin medic. That decided that. He reached out and pushed the bell.

The faint tone sounded from inside, and the door opened with a faint swish. There she was.

Slight, with pale blonde hair and delicate features, Sharah stood there decked out in a pair of blue jeans and a pretty peasant top.

Chase blinked. He was used to seeing her in her scrubs, so this was new for him. But then she smiled and invited him in, and he was suddenly inside her apartment and the flowers were in her hands, and she was showing him to the sofa.

"Have a seat. Would you like something to drink? Some wine or coffee or...I don't know what you like." Sharah paused, blushing. "I just realized, I have no idea what you like to do after work. Other than hang out with Delilah and her family." She bit her lip, blushing again. "I'm sorry—I realize you may not want to talk about..." Dropping to the sofa, she let out a sigh. "I'm blowing it, aren't I? This was probably a bad idea and I'm sorry I started it. I don't even know what to call you."

Chase grinned, then. The pale rose of her cheeks touched his heart, and she seemed so delicate, yet so steady in herself. He wanted to help her out, to put her at ease. "How about Chase? And no, this wasn't a bad idea. Terribly awkward, yes, but I think we both knew it was going to be that. Let's face it, this puts us on new territory, Sharah. I guess we take it one step at a time."

She took a deep breath and let it out slowly. "Okay. Let's start over. First, let me put these in some water. Do you want something to drink?" She paused by the door leading into the kitchen, flowers in hand.

Chase was about to offer to help her, but then he thought that maybe she wanted a moment to compose herself, so he forced himself to remain seated. "Yeah, a cup of coffee would be nice. Black, with one sugar, please."

As she disappeared, he looked around. The living room had a Victorian feel to it—there were delicate bric-a-brac scattered around, porcelain figurines of dancing women, and of frogs and raccoons, of all things. A heavy wooden frame that was painted gold held a picture over the fireplace, and he recognized it as a copy of J.W. Waterhouse's Boreas. The girl in the painting could have passed for one of the Fae, or an elf, caught in a blustery wind as her shawl billowed around her. Plants grew everywhere, from aloe to potted herbs to unusual flowers Chase had never seen, but that he knew must have come from Otherworld.

He tried to relax. Sharah was his friend. She was a damned good worker—the head medic—and technically, she really didn't work for him, but more...alongside him. He couldn't really fire her unless she did something horrendous. The medical division of the Faerie-Human Crime Scenes Investigation unit was mostly autonomous, though they worked in synch—and often answered to—the law enforcement division.

Another moment and Sharah returned, tray in hand. She slid it onto the table and poured him a mug. As she handed it to him, their fingers touched and a brief spark flared. Chase pulled away so fast he almost spilled the steaming coffee all over him.

"So..." All of a sudden, every thought in his head vanished and he had no clue what he was going to say.

"It was a slow day today—only four injuries." Sharah stopped herself, biting her lip. She glanced over at him. "Um...your turn."

Chase fingered the neck of his collar, pulling on it. He felt on trial—almost as nervous as when he'd interviewed for his job. "Same here...except..." He was about to say something about Delilah and one of the demons, but decided that wasn't the wisest move. Delilah was out of the picture now, out of his life except as a friend, but that didn't mean her name didn't come with a buttload of baggage for both himself and Sharah.

They sat there for a moment, again not speaking, and Chase thought that perhaps this was the worst date ever. But at that moment, his cell phone rang. Relieved, he answered. It was Yugi.

"Boss, we have a problem. There's a fight going on in the morgue and we need you back here—Sharah too." Yugi was the only one at the station who knew that Chase and Sharah were giving the dating thing a chance.

"We're on our way." Chase punched the End Talk button. "Yugi said there's..." He stopped. "A fight in the morgue? What the hell?" He jumped up. "We're both needed at the station. Come on, I'll give you a ride."

She looked just about as relieved as he felt, and grabbed her purse and coat. "I'm ready. Let me turn off the coffeemaker first."

As she ducked into the kitchen, Chase stared morosely at the sofa. This had been a bad idea. He was sure of it. There was no way in hell that he and Sharah could make anything work between them.

Of that, he was sure.

YUGI WAS FRANTIC, and Yugi was hardly ever frantic. When Chase and Sharah rushed through the door, he let out a mumbled, "Thank heavens" and motioned for them to follow him to the elevator.

"What happened?" Chase checked his service weapon, making sure it was firm in his holster. He held the elevator door for Sharah, then entered the car. As the doors swished shut, Yugi leaned against the railing, looking exhausted.

"We had a problem in the morgue. I don't know what practical joker decided to get a leg up on us, but we brought in three bodies tonight—car crash. Supes involved, we were told. I was wrapping up the reports for the day when I get a summons from the morgue. Big problem, Clyde says—the bodies aren't dead."

"What do you mean?" Sharah asked. "Should I get up to the ER?"

Yugi shook his head. "No, they weren't injured either."

"Vampires rising?" *Please, oh please, don't let it be vamps*, Chase thought. The last thing he felt like doing tonight was taking on a pack of newly minted vampires.

Once again, Yugi shook his head. "Nope. Seems a couple of the local teens—Earthside Fae— thought it would be funny to stage a car crash and...well...long story short, the victims are actually zombies. Somehow they devised a stasis spell that kept the zombies from moving. They're fresh enough that it fooled the medic."

"You have to be kidding." Chase stared at him. Teenaged humans were bad enough, but he had discovered that teen Supes could be far, far worse.

"I wish I was. Once the bodies were here, as Clyde and his assistant were opening the body bags, the spell wore off and the zombies started moving. Clyde and Jeffrey managed to get out without being hurt, but the zombies are in there causing havoc. And we were going to put them down, except for the fact that we're not sure whose bodies they are, when they were killed—for all we know they may be fresh kills—and...I thought I'd better call you."

Sharah let out a disgusted grumble. "If we catch the idiots, I'd like to have ten minutes alone with them."

Chase glanced at her. "Take 'em down a peg, huh?"

She snorted. "You have not seen how elfin children are disciplined. Oh, no abuse, but a stupid stunt like this would warrant six months of community service and an ass whipping."

"You know this for a fact, do you?" Chase let out a grin as the doors opened and they stepped out of the elevator.

"I'll have you know, I did far worse when I was younger—and yes, that is a standard punishment. I still have the memories to prove it." Sharah laughed. "I wasn't always the upstanding medic-healer I am now." She winked at him and Chase's stomach fluttered at the coy gleam in her eye. Maybe...maybe...

Yugi stopped in front of the doors leading into the general morgue. "I'm not sure what to do. How do we subdue them so we can identify the bodies before we...um..."

"Destroy them?" Chase frowned. "Good question. We could drive them into a cell and lock them up."

"Yeah, but that entails getting them upstairs to the holding tanks." Yugi shrugged. "I really don't feel like acting bait."

Sharah let out a sigh. "I suppose that's where I come in, right? You're wondering if there are any drugs that will sedate a zombified body?"

Yugi nodded. "Well, actually, yes."

"You're in luck." She stopped by one of the hall phones. "Let me call upstairs and have Arralyn bring it down."

Yugi motioned Chase aside. "I'm so sorry for interrupting your evening. We just didn't know what to do and—"

"No worries, man. I think we both welcomed the interruption." Chase hadn't intended on spilling the beans, but he was so disappointed that he couldn't keep it out of his voice. "I don't think the date was a good idea."

Yugi cocked his head. "But you guys are great together—you get along, you have a similar sense of humor, and I know Sharah's attracted to you."

"That's all well and good but we had nothing to talk about—shush. Here she comes." Chase

stopped talking as Sharah returned to their con-
clave. "Arralyn on the way?"

"Yes, he's bringing down several doses now. Be
very careful—if even a drop of this stuff gets in
the blood stream of someone who's alive, it can
paralyze the lungs. Which translates to: deader
than a doornail." She suddenly stopped and turned
toward the door of the morgue. "Guys, we have
company."

At that point, the door opened and the three
zombies shambled out. They were definitely dead,
that much was apparent, and not all that long ago.
Chase started to reach for his gun but then remembered that zombies really didn't respond to being shot. They were already dead, and the bullets
didn't do much to put a stop to them. At that point,
he also realized that the hallway wasn't all that big
and the only way out was through the other side
of the morgue to the stairwell, or back into the
elevator. And getting to the stairwell would require
going *through* the zombies.

"Unless one of you has an axe, I suggest retreat!"
He grabbed Sharah's arm and turned to race
toward the elevator. Yugi was right on their heels.
But the zombies were entirely too fast and the
elevator seemed to be hung up on one of the other
floors.

Chase swore. He didn't remember zombies being
this fast. He glanced around. There were two doors
in the hallway—one was to a restroom, the other
to the janitor's closet. Yugi was already hightailing
it for the janitor's closet, but now one of the zombies was too close and if Chase and Sharah tried to

join him, they'd be within striking range. Sharah grabbed Chase's hand and made a mad dash for the restroom. As soon as they were inside, she hit the lights and locked the door, leaning against it as one of the zombies began to beat against it.

"Thank gods this is a one-person stall," she said, looking around. "Otherwise it wouldn't have a lock on it and we'd be hip-deep in trouble."

Chase looked around. Usually bathrooms in medical facilities had phones, but this was the morgue level and there was no need for that—the patients didn't usually get up and attack the technicians. He looked around for someplace to sit, but the only choice was the toilet and somehow, that seemed so indecorous.

Sharah seemed to notice what he was doing. "Oh go ahead. I don't care."

Grateful, he lowered the seat and sat on the john. "Thanks. I guess I'd better call upstairs for some help." He pulled out his cell phone and punched in the front desk's number. A few minutes later, he glanced back at Sharah, who was studiously ignoring the grunts on the other side of the door. "They'll be down as soon as they can get the manpower. Right now, nobody upstairs has ever fought a zombie and Arralyn isn't about to come down here with the drug without an escort. So we're stuck here for a while."

Sharah let out snicker. "Well, you have to admit, this is turning out to be one of the worst dates ever."

Chase winced. "I know, and I'm sorry. I don't know what happened at your place. I choked, I guess. Everything seemed so strange and awkward, all of a sudden."

Sharah laughed. "You felt that way too? I thought it was just me. All I could think about was, oh my gods, I'm dating the man who hired me and how the hell can I compare to his last girlfriend?"

Chase blinked. It never occurred to him that she would compare herself to Delilah. "You've got to be kidding. You're worried about me comparing you to Delilah?"

Sharah glanced down at the floor and her smile vanished, replaced by a nervous twitch of the lip. "Well...she's...look at what she and her sisters do. She's incredibly athletic, she can turn into a cat and a panther, and...she fights demons. I'm just an elfin medic. I kind of wonder...why you broke up with her? Why did you ask me out?" And right there, her voice cracked and she covered her face. "I can't believe I just said that. You must think I'm horrible—but..."

Chase slid down on the floor next to her, his nervousness forgotten. "I had no clue you felt that way." He reached out and took her hands. Overhead, the zombies were at it again, thudding against the door. "Will you shut up out there, you freaks?"

Sharah laughed then—not much but it was a start. "I don't think they're going to pay much attention to you, even if you do have a badge."

Chase snorted. "Not that many people do anyway." He sobered. "Seriously, I wish I had known you felt this way before. I could have...okay, just... ask me whatever you want. Please."

She blinked, and the blue of her eyes touched his heart. They were soft, and caring, and he realized just how incredibly sexy she looked with her hair streaming down the sides of her face. She was blonde, like Delilah, but she was also...different. A vulnerability there that she couldn't hide.

"Okay. Why did you break up with Delilah?"

Chase licked his lips. "I haven't told anybody this. The only one who knows is Delilah herself—and probably her sisters. What one knows, the others do. I love those girls—I really do. But Delilah needs someone who isn't going to constantly want to run to her rescue. I always want to be that guy. Don't get me wrong, I love strong women, but I don't think I can ever be the kind of guy who can go out there at the front of the pack with her. I'm human. I'm a cop, not a warrior. There's a difference."

Sharah nodded, soberly. "In Elqaneve, we have a saying. *Thinkers plan the wars. Warriors fight the battles. Without one, the other cannot function.* Both are necessary, and both have their places. But it's hard for a thinker...a planner...to match pace with a warrior—and vice versa. Sometimes it works, but sometimes the differences are too great." She paused, then cocked her head to one side. "Is that the only reason?"

Chase smiled gently, taking her hand. "No, I didn't break up with her just because I can't run to her rescue. I'd be a poor excuse for a man if that were the only reason. Ever since I was given the Nectar of Life, I've been changing. I can't...the future seems so nebulous now. Before, I had it all planned out and now—conceivably, I have a thousand years ahead of me. I have no clue what that might bring. It's not that I don't want to commit to a relationship, but Delilah...a thousand years...I don't think it would work for us."

"If your heart tells you that it was the right decision, it's good you paid attention." She paused, then shook her head. "Wait...did you say you broke up with *her*?"

Chase grinned. "You thought she broke up with me, didn't you? And that I'm nursing unrequited love and regret?"

Sharah blushed and covered her face with her hands, laughing. "I admit it—yes, I did. I thought I was—"

"A rebound fling?"

"Something like that."

Chase scooted over so that he could slide his arm around her shoulders. She leaned against him and it felt like a perfect fit. "Sharah, I never ask anybody out on the rebound. And I never ask anybody out that I don't find attractive, or interesting." He tipped her head up so she was staring him in the eyes. "I asked you out because I like you, because you're lovely and talented and...because I wanted to do this." Slowly, he leaned down and pressed his lips against hers. As he sunk into the kiss, the scent of orange blossom and honeysuckle coiled around him and he lost himself in the feel of her soft body pressed against his. Eventually, someone would come destroy the zombies, but for now, he thought, the morgue bathroom seemed like the perfect place to get to know one another.

Ink Bonds

There was a point where Trillian realized he needed to seek out Camille again, and he was determined to find her, if it was the last thing he ever did.

TRILLIAN STRODE THROUGH the city. Y'Elestrial hadn't changed a lot since he'd last been here, but he had. Last time he left, he swore never to come back. When Camille had rejected him, he'd pursued her, begged her to reconsider, but she had shut him out and refused to see him. Even though they were connected by an unbreakable bond, she'd pushed him away and sequestered herself in her house. So, he had walked out of the city, angry and seething. That had been twelve years ago, and during all that time, he had thought about her every day. Every time he touched another woman, he saw Camille's face. Every time he heard a throaty laughter, he'd turned around, hoping to see her standing there. But he never thought he'd step back inside the gates of Y'Elestrial. Until he was hired for a mission that he couldn't refuse.

TRILLIAN STARED UP at the palace, then back at the orders in his hand. The name brought back both bad memories and good ones.

Darynal clapped his back. Trillian had asked his blood oath brother to come with him because otherwise, he wasn't sure he'd have the courage to go through with it. "You okay? You still want to do this?"

Trillian nodded. "Yeah, but to tell you the truth, I'm not sure what I expect." His gaze rose, following the spires of the ostentatious palace. "I don't even know if she's here. And if she is...will her father even tell her I'm here?"

"How long has it been since you've seen each other?" Darynal crossed his arms over his chest, shivering as a gust of wind blew past. It was getting chilly—autumn was well under way and it wouldn't be more than a moon or two before the snows would cover the land.

Trillian let out a soft sigh. "Which time? We broke up so many times it's hard to count. But the last time—before she shut me out completely—was a couple years ago. We were meeting in secret before that. We never could keep away from each other. But finally, she walked away from me." His heart ached, though he wouldn't tell anybody but he knew that Darynal could sense it. Darynal was like he was—an outcast, though it might not appear so to those who weren't privy to the inner workings of the Svartan race.

Darynal nodded. "What are you afraid will happen?"

"That I won't find her. That her father will turn me away." Trillian paused, then shuddered. "That she'll be there and I'll talk to her and..." And... what? What did he really fear? Was he so afraid that Camille would refuse to hear him out? Or was he afraid that she might say yes, might listen. That their passion might come cascading back? Because if it did, he wasn't sure that he could go through another breakup. The last time had been almost too much to handle."There's only one way to find out, man. Come on." Darynal started walking toward the palace.

After a moment, Trillian joined him. The message he carried had to be delivered one way or another, and he might as well get it over with. The orders weighed heavily in his hand, and not just because they were addressed to Sephreh ob Tanu—Camille's father. No, Trillian had managed a peek in them, even though they were supposedly sealed. He was very good with ferreting out information when he needed to. And what was within this scroll could shake the world if they knew.

"What did your father say when you hired on with Queen Asteria?" Darynal knew just the thing to take Trillian's mind off his impending meeting, and that was to bring up something conceivably worse.

Trillian gave him a scathing look. "What do you think he said? I was already walking on thin ice. They never accepted me even before I met Camille and it's gone downhill since then. Even when we broke up, my father said I had shamed the family too much. When I accepted the commission with Elqaneve, he told me to leave and never darken his doorway again. He revoked my standing, erased me from the family tree, and took away my name. That's why I started using Zanzera—my aunt Leelee said I could take her name. She was cut off by the main branch of the family, too."

Darynal nodded. "I think I met Leelee once, didn't I?"

"Yes, when we stopped for dinner that one time on a hunting trip? Remember I asked you not to mention it to my parents? If they had known that I stepped over the threshold in Leelee's house, I would have gotten the hiding of my life." Trillian wiped one hand across his eyes. There were so many politics to worry about at home. It had almost been a relief when his father had turned him away for good.

The palace was spacious and ornate to the point of being gaudy. Lethesanar liked her opium, and she liked her bling, and the more addicted she grew to the drug, the more lavish her spending became. The stirrings in the underground were that war was in the offing. Rumors had it that Tanaquar—Lethesanar's sister who had vanished some years back—had banded together with an army and that they were planning a coup. But rumors could be wrong, and best to work with the powers that be, rather than the powers that might never come to the throne. At least until the changeover.

Trillian was a pragmatist. He'd watched friends get mowed under when they chose the wrong cause, the wrong side, the wrong battle. And now that Svartalfheim was getting ready to relocate to Otherworld from the Subterranean Realms, everything was up in the air. Turmoil was the name of the game, and he watched every move he made. That was the way to survive, and Trillian had been in some dicey spots before.

As he and Darynal lightly ran up the steps to the central doors, Trillian flashed back to the last time he'd seen Camille—their last parting.

"I CAN'T BELIEVE you are doing this again. How many times do I have to tell you, I am not like the rest of my people?" Trillian couldn't believe they were here again. How many times had they stood at this point, and how many times had either he or Camille stormed out, ending their relationship *for good*?

"I know what blood is like. I know how your family feels about me—about us. Eventually, you're going to get tired of running from them. You're going to want to go home and claim your inheritance. And I can't go with you. I can't live in the Subterranean Realms, and I can't...I can't live with people who hate me. I get enough of that here from my own relatives." Camille dropped into a chair, rocking as she hugged herself tightly. Her hair trailed down her back, a cloak of raven curls. She gazed up at him, her eyes pale and flashing. She had been running magic heavily the past month, and the violet of her irises was almost eclipsed with the silver flecks.

Trillian wanted to tell her that his father had thrown him out—he wanted to tell her that he hardly ever saw his family, but his pride was still stinging, and the truth was, he wanted her to accept him as is, with all his flaws, including his family. After all, he accepted her father hating him. He let out a long sigh and sat down on the bench opposite her. "You know I would never cast you off. I know what this is about. It's about Rona."

Rona...the name weighed heavily on his thoughts. Rona was the woman his family had chosen for him to marry. They had made it clear that he was of age now and if he ever expected to inherit his share of the family fortune, he would come home and marry the King's niece. "You can bring your half-human whore, if you like, but she'll always be in your stable. You can never marry her and you'd better accept that now."

And so, he had run once again, hoping to stave off the argument till later, and he hadn't bothered to mention it to Camille, hoping to keep her from worrying. But he hadn't counted on how cagey his mother was. She'd sent a messenger to Camille, telling her about the marriage and how Camille could never expect to be anything but Trillian's lower-caste mistress.

And now, here they were.

Camille stared at him, tears trailing down her face. "I never expected to be monogamous—I don't know if I can be. But I will never settle for playing second fiddle. And I will never live in a house that considers me a common whore."

Trillian reached out to wipe away the tears but she flinched. "I will never ask you to do that. You know that. I have no intentions on marrying Rona, or any other woman except you. But I can't live here either, not with your father's scorn. Come away with me. We'll make our lives somewhere free from family and duty." But even as he said it, he knew it was a death knell, because he knew Camille.

She straightened her shoulders. As she wiped her eyes, her expression slid into a mute, painful acceptance. "You know I can't do that. You know that I have my sisters to look after—Menolly is still finding her way now. You remember how horrible that time was—Father still hasn't recovered. And Delilah needs me. And...I am—"

"A guardsman's daughter. I know, I know. I've heard it so much I can recite it in my sleep." Even though he didn't mean it to come out snarky, it did. Apparently that was exactly the wrong thing to say.

Camille slowly stood. "You've always lived by your own rules. But you know who I am, and if it pains you so much, then why are you still here?"

Trillian desperately wanted to take it back, but it was too late. Some words cannot be unsaid, and he'd crossed the line. Her family was fucked up—

there was no denying that—but he knew that the only way Camille had to deal with the loss of her mother, the way her sister had been turned and abused, and the reserve of her father was to put her duty and honor at the forefront. It kept her going, it gave her something to hold on to because gods knew, there wasn't much else for her to lean on.

"I'm so sorry..." He fumbled for words.

"How many times have we done this?" She slowly crossed to the bed where her cloak was lying, neatly folded. "How many times have we had this argument? If it wasn't Rona, it was always something else that set it off."

"Camille—don't do anything you'd regret. Please, calm down." Trillian stepped closer, trying to embrace her, but she held out her arm.

"I think it's time we just called it for what it is—a giant mistake."

"We're bound. You can't just walk out on me. I love you, and you love me. I know this—can you deny it?" He was desperate now, wishing to hell he could have kept a hold of his tongue. And he wanted to lash his mother—she'd set this up.

But Camille just let out a strangled laugh. "Isn't that the most painful rub of all? No, I can't forget you. I can't just walk away and leave you in the dust. But I can walk toward the future. And Trillian, I think I have to walk away from you. You'll find someone else. Go marry Rona. I'm sure she won't be the hassle I am." And with that, she turned and swept out of the room before he could run after her.

Trillian considered following her, begging her to come back. And he knew he would...but a gnawing fear in the pit of his stomach told him that this had been one step too far. That they would never come back from here.

"THE CAPTAIN WILL see you now." The secretary led him into the office that he'd been dreading. Trillian found himself staring at a man who hated his guts. Who probably had hoped to never see him again.

When the door shut behind them, he remained standing at attention. Captain Sephreh stood and walked out from behind the desk, eyeing him up and down with an unreadable stare. After a moment, he held out his hand.

"You have a missive for me?"

"Yes, sir." Trillian handed Sephreh the note.

Sephreh took it, opened it, and read it, then placed it carefully in his pocket. As he slowly returned to his desk, he said, "That will be all. You may go."

Trillian hesitated. It would be rude to ignore the order, even though he was no Guard Des'Estar, nor a member of the OIA, but he couldn't just walk out. Not without asking.

"Captain..."

Sephreh turned slowly, staring at him with an icy glint. "What do you want, Trillian? Why did you come back? I can't believe you give a damn about this mission, or anything Queen Asteria asked you to do. What are you looking for?"

Trillian stiffened. Truth was, he really didn't care much about what he was doing, though he'd keep his word—once he was paid for a mission, he made it a point to follow through. After a pause, he finally decided he might as well just come to the point.

"I'm looking for Camille. I have to talk to her. Where is she?"

Sephreh let out a snort. "You think I'd lead you to my daughter? I rejoiced the day she came to her senses and finally sent you packing. You're not welcome in my family, Zanzera. Know that right now."

"Your family doesn't concern me, but Camille does. She and I have been through the Eleshinar ritual together. We are bound and if I'm hurting this much without her, she's going to be hurting without me." Trillian tossed his messenger bag on a chair and strode forward, leaning across Sephreh's desk. "I love your daughter and I cannot forget her. You can hate me all you want, but you're not the one who I care about."

Sephreh jumped up, his eyes flashing. He looked so much like Camille that it tore at Trillian's gut. Like daughter, like father when it came to temper, that was for sure.

"I dismissed you!"

"And I refuse to be dismissed so easily." Trillian slammed his hand on the desk. "Where is she? If she still wants nothing to do with me, I'll walk out of her life again, but I will not leave without talking to her!"

And then, Sephreh began to laugh. He dropped back into his chair. "Good luck, then." His gaze was still cold as steel, but he looked positively delighted.

"What do you mean?"

"Camille no longer lives in Otherworld. She's gone Earthside—relocated by the OIA. My daughter is now an agent over through the portals. So good luck finding her." As he chuckled, he pulled the letter out of his pocket. "By the way, I'll have my response to Queen Asteria by morning. You may drop by to pick it up on your way back to Elqaneve. I trust you won't be staying in Y'Elestrial any longer than necessary." And with that pointed remark, he nodded to the door. "See yourself out, Zanzera. I'm busy."

As Trillian stumbled back toward the door, grabbing his bag on the way, he couldn't help but wonder just how the hell he was supposed to find Camille now. She was over Earthside. She might as well be a million miles away.

DARYNAL STARED AT him as they crowded into the palace cafeteria that served the agents and soldiers from the various departments of the government. The city-state might be a monarchy, but it had its layers of bureaucracy like all governments.

"She's over Earthside? What are you going to

do?"

Trillian pushed the stew around on his plate. He frowned. "I have one possible chance. I know someone who works in the OIA, in communications. I think I can get him to help me."

"What are you going to do? Head over there?" Darynal started to laugh, then stopped. "Oh man, you can't. You are actually thinking of traveling through the portals?"

"It's not like I haven't been Earthside before. I've been there several times on missions. I know my way around enough." He knew it sounded crazy—to shift worlds in order to chase down someone likely to slam the door in his face. But he had to find her. He had to know. "Come on. I've got an appointment with Leks. He's waiting."

The two men entered the communications hive a few minutes later, and there was Leks, waiting. The room was filled with Whispering Mirrors, all pointing to locations around Y'Elestrial and far beyond. The silver rimmed magical devices were hard to tune, and it required an entire department to keep them up and running.

Leks glanced around, then—with no one paying any attention—led them over to one bank of mirrors. "I'll lose my job if anybody finds out about this. But here...the D'Artigo Sisters are in a city called Seattle, over Earthside. Their contact's name is Chase Johnson. He's a soldier...officer? Someone in authority, that I know. He's the one who all communications from the OIA go through officially. The girls have a Whispering Mirror in their house but I haven't figured out just the combination for their location yet. This will have to do on such short notice."

As they came up on the mirror, he motioned for the man keeping an eye on the bank of mirrors to take a break. "I want to check something out. Go get your tea early."

The apprentice didn't have to be asked twice. He saluted and headed off, looking decidedly more happy than he had when they'd approached him.

Leks looked around, then sat down and fiddled with the controls on the mirror. He whispered something that neither Trillian nor Darynal could hear—a password, no doubt. Within a moment, the cloud obscuring the mirror began to fade, and there was a man staring back at them.

"Yes? What can I do for you?" The man looked nervous, and kept tugging on his collar.

He was clean cut, with hair shorter than just about anybody Trillian had ever seen. He looked decidedly human, but there was something...a faint glimmer that aroused a suspicion in the Svartan. He ignored it, though, because he had only a few minutes and he didn't want to waste any time. As Leks began to talk to the man, Trillian thought about what he was going to say. If he pled for Camille to hear him out, it would be via this human, and second hand love letters were no better than the person relaying them. No, he had to make it something that would catch her attention, that would be something she couldn't ignore.

And then, he knew. What he'd read in the note—it would concern her, too.

"I'll be back in a moment, Chase. Just wait here,

please." Leks stood and quickly walked around behind the mirror. He nodded to Trillian.

Trillian slid into the seat and leaned forward. "Chase Johnson? You know Camille D'Artigo?"

Chase blinked, looking confused. "Yeah, who are you? What do you want?"

"Never mind that. Camille will know if you tell her what I look like. Meanwhile, I have a message for her, and I'll twist your balls off if she doesn't get it."

The man named Chase stiffened, his eyes narrowing. He cleared his throat. "Are you with the OIA?""Never you mind. Get yourself something to write with—just do it."

Chase held up a funny looking quill and a pad of paper. Trillian was acquainted with pens, so he just nodded. "Good. Now you tell Camille this: Rumor has it something big is going down in the lower depths. There's a new ruler, and he's far more ambitious than than the Beasttägger was. Don't count on help from home." He paused, asking Chase to repeat the message back to him.

"Is that all?" Chase was sounding disgruntled, but he was paying attention. He seemed to sense Trillian's urgency.

"No, tell Camille that Shadow Wing's in charge now. And he's on the warpath."

At that moment, there was a sound from behind him, and Trillian turned to see Sephreh standing there, staring at him. Without a word, he stood and followed the Captain back to his office, Darynal behind him.

"YOU ARE BANISHED from the city for three moon's time," Sephreh pointed to Darynal. "Go, now, and be glad I don't toss you in jail." He waited until the Svartan clapped Trillian on the shoulder and silently left the room.

Trillian knew where to find him, so he merely raised a hand in farewell. As soon as his blood-oath brother had left the room, he turned back to the Captain. "If you're going to flog me or flay me or whatever else you'd like to do, get it over with."

"I cannot believe the effrontery...the gall..." Sephreh sputtered for a moment, then a crafty smile crossed his face. "Oh, I won't flay you or flog you. No. You want so bad to watch over my daughter? To talk to her? Good luck. I doubt she'll give you the time of day."

"What do you mean?" Trillian cocked his head to the side.

"You want to find her? Then go. Through the portals, you demon. Go over Earthside and see how long you last. Go tell my daughter I sent you as a messenger boy, to watch over her." Sephreh paused, then—with a glance at his office door, which was closed—he said, "You're right. Shadow Wing is on the rise. We've been aware of this for a while, but there are so many facets we cannot do anything openly about it. So you go, spawn from the realms, and you keep an eye on what happens to the portals over there. If my daughter will talk to you, fine—her choice. But I give you a chance in hell that she'll ever speak to you again. She knows her duty. I trust her to remain true to her head. My guess is you'll be dead in no time. You can't make it over Earthside. I was there years back, and it's far harder now. An arrogant turncoat like you? I give you thirty days."

Trillian extended his hand. "I wager you a bet, ob Tanu. If I survive that long, you shake my hand and buy me a beer. If not, you win."

Sephreh stared at Trillian's fingers. He let out a soft snort. "I'll never sully my flesh by touching yours. My daughter may have been a fool, but trust me, she's come to her senses since being sent over Earthside. Now go. And if I don't hear that you reported to Milligan at the portals by sunset, your head is forfeit and you will die. Go."

As Trillian turned on his heel and left the office, he realized the captain had played right into his hands. With a soft laugh, he whispered, "I take your bet and raise it, Sephreh. Not only will I find Camille, I guarantee you this: I'll never lose her again." His heart skipped a beat as he headed for the portals. His family be damned, Sephreh be damned. He was on his way to see his love. They were bound by a ritual as old as time, and the hidden tattoos that lurked beneath their skin would hold them together forever. And this time, nothing in the world could keep them apart.

Blood Ties

Roman has managed to live as long as he has due to keeping a tight hold on what humanity he has left. Unfortunately, not all vampires feel that way—and not all of his family feels agrees with him.

ROMAN STARED AT the phone as he silently replaced the receiver. The news was not good. He really, really didn't need to start off the day this way. Grumbling, he stared at the woman sitting beside him. She was quiet, polite, and dressed in a dark red skirt and top. *The better not to show stains,* my dear, he thought. He contemplated her—she was new to his stable. Average build, pretty, blue-eyed and a redhead. As he looked at her, it occurred to him that, for once, he wished he could have a normal breakfast and a normal cup of coffee. *Just once.* But those simple joys had been off his table for thousands of years and the only way he could handle everything that seemed so alien now, that made up so much of so many peoples' lives, was to push the desire aside and not let it bother him.

"What's your name?" Roman made it a point to know every bloodwhore in his stable. He learned their backgrounds, their likes and dislikes, the reason they had petitioned to join his household. He was not a *use 'em and lose 'em* type of guy. It wouldn't be seemly, not for the son of Blood Wyne, the Vampire Queen.

"Dotti Rollins." She smiled, but behind the smile, her nerves were showing through. She was dressed like Roman preferred his stable to dress—skirts, sweaters, normal clothes. He never allowed one of his bloodwhores to appear at the table in anything but a tidy manner. No negligees, no lingerie. Sexy clothes were perfectly fine, but he wasn't running a brothel and the fact was, he rarely slept with any of the women who lived under his roof and provided him with their blood.

Roman considered her for a moment. She seemed pleasant, almost college-prep. What was she doing here? What had brought her into his house, into his stable? He left the choosing of the bloodwhores up to his personal secretary but this meeting—the first—was the final decision. Here, he either put his stamp of approval on the deal, or he dismissed the candidates and they were never allowed to reapply.

"Tell me about yourself, Dotti." Roman was gracious. He could afford to be. There were a long line of applicants waiting to offer their veins up to him. It had been so very long, so many thousands of years, since he was human that he'd forgotten whatever it was he'd felt about vampires before his mother was turned, and in turn—turned him and his siblings. But he kept a tight, short rein on himself to keep from becoming a monster. To keep from hating his existence. And that included interacting with the living on a gracious, if aloof, level. As far above them as he was on the food chain, he never let himself forget that he did have his vulnerabilities, and death—the final death—was always a chance.

Her eyes went wide and she flushed. "I'm...I'm a grad student.

He nodded. There was something there, below the surface. "What's your major?"

This time the flush ran down her neck, across the top of her chest. "Supe-psychology."

And there it was. He knew there was something odd about her. Usually the ones who really wanted to be here were broken in some manner—they might hide it well, but the sense was always there beneath the surface. Dotti wanted fodder for her thesis. Roman could handle the broken ones. It was almost a service, offering them shelter and protection. But he didn't like being used, nor analyzed.

He slowly stood and crossed to her side, reaching down to cup her chin and slowly tilt her head up so she was looking into his eyes. He thought about just sending her away, but then the hunger grew, and he decided what the hell. He could send her away afterward. Leaning down, he brushed her lips with one finger.

"Well, Dotti, I hope you get everything you're looking for." And then, he lifted her hair away from her neck and with one, smooth motion, slid his fangs into the flesh—deep and painfully. She cried out and stiffened as he coaxed the blood up, and then, he decided to give her a taste of the other side. Within seconds she was murmuring at his touch, moaning gently as he poured on the glamour. A moment later and she squirmed, reaching up to brush her fingers across her breasts. One more lick of the blood running down her neck and she came, harder than she'd ever come before. Roman knew the signs. Dotti had never felt the wave of passion he was surrounding her with. As he pulled away, he thought with regret that she'd never feel it again, either. Not unless she knelt at his feet and begged. But he didn't like sycophants, and so even if she did, he'd just say no.

He slowly withdrew, delicately tapping his face with a napkin. "Dotti?"

She blinked, coming out of haze into which he'd thrust her. "Yes, Lord Roman?"

"Gather your things and leave my house. I don't ever want to see you again." And with that, he turned, and strode out of the room, leaving her behind. The day had started rotten and was just getting worse.

AS ROMAN LEANED toward his computer, glancing over the monthly summaries his secretary had provided him, he paused, his thoughts drifting. Every tap at the door put him on alert. Why hadn't Caleb given him time to bug out of the country? He thought about doing just that, leaving now and pretending he'd missed the letter this morning, but Blood Wyne would know, and when his mother got bug up her butt, there was no stopping her.

Finally, he pushed aside all the business matters that were on his calendar. He had already made one call he hadn't wanted to and promptly at seven, the door opened and Menolly and Nerissa walked in. Neither one looked thrilled to be here, and he couldn't blame them.

"I'm sorry I ruined your evening. I know you had plans." Roman stood, bowing gracefully. A little courtesy went a long way. "I wouldn't have called you if I had any choice in the matter but family..."

Menolly snorted. "Dude, my family's dysfunctional. Yours is downright scary. They call, you jump." She turned to Nerissa. "You understand, right?"

Nerissa nodded at Roman. Her eyes were fixated on his, and he felt himself pull back. He would never tell anyone, but the person in this world that frightened him most, among the living, was Nerissa—Menolly's wife. She alone saw him as a rival, and rivals often ended up dead. But he'd made a promise to his official consort that he'd never hurt the werepuma, and he would keep that promise. Above all, Roman was a man of his word—honor meant everything to him.

Those lovely pink lips had been around his cock once, in an ill-fated threesome that he tried to forget. His heart made it difficult, though, because he was as smitten with Menolly as Nerissa was, but he also knew it was hopeless to try to win her away. But one day the werepuma would age and die, and he and Menolly would still live and then...then he would make his move. Until then, they would play the game by the rules that the girls had set forth.

"My brother will be here shortly. He's Regent over in western Europe—France, Spain, Italy, and a few smaller countries. He insisted on meeting you. Mother told him about us." Even the words 'my brother' left a bad taste in Roman's mouth. He didn't like his siblings—they were whiny and annoying, they pranced around like royalty instead of assuming an air of dignity. Blood Wyne kept reminding him that they were always like that, even before she'd turned them, but to Roman, that didn't make an excuse for keeping up the behavior.

"As long as he doesn't touch Nerissa." Menolly brushed back Nerissa's hair. She'd affixed a pink bow around the werepuma's neck, tied in the front, which meant "*hands off, I own her.*"

"Even those of the nobility, with the exception of my mother, have to follow the rules." Roman smoothly slid from behind his desk and crossed. He lifted Nerissa's hand to his lips and gently kissed the top. She didn't flinch, but merely inclined her head to him. And *that* made him more nervous than he had thought possible.

As they stood there, an odd little trio, a knock

sounded on the door, eclipsing any thoughts of
Nerissa. Roman's stomach tightened. Just because
he was dead, didn't mean he couldn't feel sick to
his stomach. He motioned for the women to sit
near the desk, then took his place behind the behemoth of an oak antique. After straightening his
smoking jacket and smoothing back his pony tail,
pressed the button that gave the servants leave to
enter the room.

The maid entered, her eyes wide and looking
afraid. Behind her was a hooded and cloaked figure, at least six feet tall, wearing a blood red cloak,
with gold trim. The cloak was rich velvet, fastened
by a brooch that Roman recognized. He had one
like it, as well as a cloak that was the same. The
cloaks were handmade, only for their family. The
tailor had in the family since Roman could first
remember. Blood Wyne had turned him, along
with a handful of servants, when she had turned
her children.

Roman inclined his head, bowing but only
slightly in a stiff, formal pose. "Caleb, you grace
my home with your presence." What he wanted to
say was *get the fuck out*, but that didn't seem to be
the most diplomatic move and his mother would
get an earful if he was rude, and then he would get
yelled at and it would be one big mess.

Caleb pushed back his hood. He was striking,
with long golden hair the color of summer sun,
and sparkling eyes the color of frost. But though
their coloring was different, the long, regal nose,
and the angular cheekbones belied their common
parentage.

Caleb glanced over at Menolly and Nerissa, his eyes flashing briefly. "Brother, it's been a long time." He wandered over to the girls, circling them. "It's easy enough to tell who your consort is."

Menolly stood and curtseyed—it was expected of her and Roman knew that it grated against her nature, but she was brought up in courtly life and understood protocol. That was main reason he had originally decided to appoint her as his official consort—that along with his mother's decree. Blood Wyne had insisted, and he still didn't know why, but things had snowballed after that and now, he was grateful for the way they'd turned out.

"How do you do, Lord Caleb." Menolly's voice was smooth, but beneath the surface, Roman could hear a rumbling of discontent.

Caleb gave her a long once-over, then turned to Nerissa. He held her gaze, but said nothing. Then, turning back to Roman, he said, "You are remiss. You offer me no one to drink?"

Roman narrowed his eyes. Caleb was up to something—he could feel it. "I am a poor host, yes. I will have a bottle of blood warmed and brought to you."

"I prefer my blood straight from the throat. You wouldn't refuse me, would you?" Caleb cleared his throat. "In fact, I'd rather you choose the woman personally. Someone who would suit all my tastes."

Roman paused. Caleb's meaning was clear. For some reason, he wanted to be alone with Menolly, and that didn't suit well. He doubted that his brother—as rough as he was—would go so far as to attack either Menolly or Nerissa, but the son of a bitch was up to something. If he capitulated, he'd leave them at risk. If he refused, he'd be branded in the court as churlish and his mother would intervene, and that could get dicey. Relative or not, she was the vampire queen, and she made her wishes known in her own time. But the one thing she was clear on: her children would follow decorum with one another, and they would break that decorum at risk to themselves and their standing in her court.

He vacillated for another moment, glancing at Menolly who shot him a confused look. Finally, Roman strode toward the door. "I'll be back with your...beverage. I'm leaving the door open. It should stay open during my absence. This is my house, and you will honor my wishes."

Caleb shrugged. "As you will.

ROMAN MOTIONED TO the one bloodwhore he knew had proclivities for masochism—actually she was a switch. In all the time he'd known his brother—which was far too long—he had also known that Caleb preferred his prey to be able to handle a little rough treatment.

"Listen," he told Renee, "I will not require you to service him if he gets out of hand. I'm having Wendy watch over you...if it gets too rough, give her the signal and she'll put a stop to it." Wendy was a vampire, tough as they come, and she guarded his stable for him.

Renee gave him a steely eyed nod. "Yes, Lord Roman. And...thank you, for watching out for me."

"I'll do the best I can but remember, this is my brother. He's one of the court. I cannot guarantee your safety but I'll do my best." Roman frowned. While he had lost a great deal of his humanity over the thousands of years, he cultivated what remained, and tried to keep himself humble enough to prevent himself from sliding fully into predator-mode. Once a vampire began to view humans—mortals—as expendable, they lost their ability to think clearly and usually found themselves very dead, very quickly. Power without restraint led to carelessness, and power without reason was a trigger to panic. And a group of panicked mortals were far more dangerous than the worst predator on the planet.

"I understand." Renee went to freshen up. Roman instructed Wendy to bring her to the office when she was ready and hurried back. He thought about calling his mother first, to find out if she had actually sent Caleb, but if she had, she might lie to him. And if she hadn't, she'd just tell him to deal with matters on his own.

As he approached the door to his office—which was still open—Roman slowed, listening. Vampires had excellent hearing. And sure enough, he heard Caleb talking.

"My brother is softer-hearted than I am, but he does a good job here. I could not be regent for this area. I prefer the Old World, where they still fear vampires enough to give us the respect we deserve.

You are telling me, you would prefer to remain here, at his side, as a consort than come with me and become a queen in your own right?"

Menolly's voice filtered out, the sultry tones vanishing from her cool, harsh reply. "Lord Caleb, your invitation is no doubt one most vampires would swoon over, but I passed swoon a long time ago. You've insulted my wife, you've insulted your brother—my consort. And you've insulted me, and then you invite me to switch sides and follow you to Europe? I have no clue how you think I'd be interested." She snorted, laughing. "Truth is? I'm from Otherworld. I'm far less tractable than women who are full-blooded human—even if they have been turned."

"You are a fool. My brother has far too many enemies and far too little gumption to wipe them out. This Vampire Nexus he seeks to create—it's a fool's dream. The humans will never accept our kind—or your kind." He must have been talking to Nerissa at that moment because she let out a harsh laugh.

"You truly think you can go back to when vampires ruled the night and people thought they were invincible? There are a thousand wannabe Buffy the Vampire Slayers out there among the hate groups and some of them are pretty damned smart. And just because my kind—Weres—are targeted too, doesn't mean we'll join you in the blood bath you seem to crave." Nerissa's voice rang indignant. Roman had heard that edge before and while he admired her willingness to stand up for what she believed, he also knew that standing up to someone like Caleb could be very, very dangerous.

Roman snarled and swung into the room. "What the hell is going on?"

Caleb jumped, his eyes turning blood red. He was glowering at Nerissa, with Menolly standing between the two, her fangs down, looking ready to strike. Nerissa was on her feet, hands on hips, glaring from behind Menolly.

Fuck, why the hell did I have to let him in the door, Roman thought. *I can handle my mother. Caleb, I simply can't trust anywhere in my city.*

"What's going on, may I ask? Caleb, why are you threatening my consort and her wife? You wouldn't be trying to steal her away, would you?" Roman sauntered in, keeping his voice light and easy. If he set Caleb off, Roman knew it would end up in a fight to the death and put the girls at risk. Caleb had a penchant for grudges and never let a slight pass by.

Caleb let out a faint snarl but pulled back. Roman glanced at Menolly and Nerissa, a warning look in his eyes, and gently shook his head, hoping they'd keep their mouths shut. Menolly started to say something but Nerissa suddenly stood and interrupted her.

"Lord Roman, our family is expecting us home—we're needed tonight and we gave our word we'd be home by nine. If we leave now, we can keep our promise." Her voice was steady and she avoided looking at Caleb, who was smoldering in his chair.

Roman gave them a brief nod. "Go then. I will not have you breaking your word."

As they gave both vampires a brief bow, Menolly

paused, looking back directly at Roman. "You know I'll never break my word." Then they disappeared out the door.

Roman waited for a moment, then turned to his brother. "What the hell was that all about? You were trying to convince my consort to leave me and go with you? And what was Nerissa talking about?"

Caleb let out a snort. "You are so good, so obedient. You follow whatever Mother says without question. And now she has been swayed—become part of the world, convince them to accept us. It will never happen. The world sees us as a plague. We're the monsters in the dark, waiting to drink their blood and turn them into monsters just like us. You and Mother think all of this..." He gestured around him. "You think the businesses and the organizations will convince mortals to leave us in peace. Fools. You're both living in a fool's paradise."

"And what are we to do otherwise? They know we exist. We either do our best to work with them or..." Roman paused. "That's what Nerissa was talking about—you intend to start a war, don't you?"

Caleb laughed. "A war? Oh, brother, the war started the first day that Kesana, the Mother of Blood, invited the demons to transform her into the first vampire. The war started back then and it will never end. I need a queen worthy to take up the battle."

Roman forced himself to hold steady, but what he wanted to do was stumble back, to grab the nearest sharp object and stake his brother. "You are mad. You would go against Blood Wyne—"

"Our mother has lost her edge. And you...what are you but a minor bureaucrat? What do you think will happen when the humans realize just how many of us there are? Do you really think they're going to let us all live? Right now, they don't realize our numbers, but you and your Nexus are intent on making us visible, and Mother has played into your hands. Menolly—I know what she's capable of. Our mother made the mistake of telling me. She'd be the perfect queen for a new realm." Caleb's eyes narrowed. They were glowing crimson now, streaked with blood, streaked with anger.

Roman knew what he should do—knew what he was obligated to do—but when it came down to it, he found himself vacillating. He'd killed countless men in battle before he'd been turned into a vampire. He'd killed countless people since then. He knew he could be ruthless, but this...fratricide, felt like a step toward finality. He'd never attacked one of his own family before. And a spark of something he hadn't felt for a long time—fear—crept into his thoughts. Caleb was strong. If he attacked him here, and didn't come out victorious, Caleb would be free, set out into Seattle without anyone to stop him.

"Go. Get out of my sight. Get out of my city." Roman whirled as a sound at the door startled both of them. There was Renee, with Wendy. "Wendy, get her out of here. Now."

Wendy obeyed immediately—she knew better

than question her master. She grabbed Renee by the arm and dragged her away.

Caleb just laughed as they left and headed toward the French doors leading out to the garden. "I'll find my refreshment elsewhere. Don't you have any worries about that. And brother," he paused, clutching the knob, "tell Mother I wish her good luck. One way or another, there will be a new queen rising, and I'm going to be right there at her side, controlling every action. The vampire nation will live again, in fury and vengeance, just like it was always meant to be."

And then, Caleb was out the door and vanished into the night. As Roman watched him go, he knew that a war was coming. If he'd tried to stop Caleb now, alone, he doubted that he could have done it. But sometime, probably sooner than later, they would meet. And Roman would have to have an army behind him, because Caleb wouldn't be coming alone. As he slowly moved to call his mother and tell her the news, he wearily thought that maybe he should just walk into the sun—be done with it and over. But that would leave Caleb free to storm against the mortals, and against Blood Wyne, and that was something Roman couldn't let happen.

As he picked up the phone, he thought, some nights seemed to last forever.

A Purr-fect Weekend

All Shade wants is a weekend alone with his Kitten...be careful of what you ask for. Sometimes you just may get it.

SHADE WAS LOOKING forward to the weekend far more than he'd looked forward to anything for a long time. He and Delilah were going to have the entire house to themselves. The family—including Maggie and Hanna—were packing up for two-day vacation out at Smoky's barrow, and he and Delilah would finally get a little time together, without anybody around. Granted, they had the entire third floor to themselves, but there was seldom a time when they had more than a few hours without an interruption. This weekend would be a wonderful cure to all of that.

He hurried down to the kitchen to say goodbye—relieved for the privacy or not, let no one ever call him churlish. And he did love the rest of the family, and felt protective of them—all dragons, half-blood or not, had that streak. It bordered on possessiveness, at times.

Camille and Menolly were in the kitchen, finishing up last minute preparations. They were leaving in the evening so Menolly could get her lair ready for sunrise deep in the barrow out by Mount Rainier. Delilah was sitting on the counter, swinging her legs back and forth.

"I wish we could go with you, but I promised Shade—" She stopped, suddenly aware he had entered the room, and blushed. "I wanted to stay..."

Shade snorted. He knew how tight the girls were. "That's all right, love. I know you want to be both places. But we planned this a few weeks ago. Please?" He turned on the puppy-dog look. He knew it would get to her and he knew that they'd have a blast once they were alone. He just had to convince her not to shift gears at the last minute.

Delilah let out a long sigh. "I know, love and... yeah, we'll have a wonderful weekend. Just us." She wrinkled her nose and hopped off the counter to give him a kiss. "I wish I could be in both places at once."

Camille grinned. "I could try a bilocation spell—I bet it would work. My magic is a lot stronger."

Both Menolly and Shade jerked around to stare at her. Shade glanced at Delilah, then shook his head. "Not a good idea, Camille. It's not that I don't trust you but..."

Delilah let out a snort. "I wish you could. I'd love to go tramping around in the woods. But..." She frowned, worrying her lip, then turned to Shade.

"Love, can you go get my backpack? I need to give Camille something that's in it. It's in the parlor."

As Menolly shouldered her bags and headed out the door, waving behind her, Shade frowned and headed back into the living room. He had the feeling that they were up to something and it didn't make him any easier that Delilah obviously didn't want him to know what. If it had just been girl talk, they would have gone right on in front of him. He was used to that by now.

The backpack was in the parlor like she'd said. Shade carried it to the kitchen, but stopped short. There, on the counter, was Delilah in her tabby form, and Camille was frowning, tapping her foot as she stared at the cat. Startled as he strode into the room, a guilty look washed across her face.

"Shade! Um...you found her backpack." Camille blushed.

Right then, he knew that something had gone down, but what? He slowly put the pack on the counter. "Why is Delilah in cat form?"

Camille cleared her throat. "We...um...Delilah, come on, shift back?" She lifted up the cat, snuggling her sister as she petted the fluffy golden puffball. Delilah's cat form was a golden tabby—furry and long haired, with a big bushy tail. She almost looked like a Maine Coon, though she wasn't quite as large as they ran. Delilah let out a purr, snuggling against Camille as she rubbed her head under her chin.

"Delilah? Delilah?" Shade frowned. Usually Delilah shifted when she was tired, or wanted to play, or when she was stressed. "Did something scare her?"

Camille refused to meet his gaze. "No. Nothing scared her. Come on, Delilah—shift back. Stop joking now."

But Delilah just wriggled in her arms and then, with a sudden leap, landed on the floor and raced into the living room. Shade swung around, staring at his sister-in-law-to-be. "What did you do, Camille?"

She sucked in a deep breath and let it out slowly. Just then, Menolly popped her head back in the door. "Camille? Are you coming?"

"I...oh hell. I'm sorry—we thought it would work." Camille glanced from Menolly to Shade, now thoroughly flustered.

"What did you think would work?" Shade rubbed his forehead. A headache was coming on. The girls were always getting themselves in one mess or another and, granted, they usually managed to dig themselves out, but this was not the way he wanted to start a romantic weekend. "Just tell me."

Menolly leaned against the wall, arms crossed, a fangy grin on her face. "I have the feeling this is going to be a good one, whatever it is."

"Oh, all right. While you were getting Delilah's pack, she asked me to try the bilocation spell on her. Apparently, it backfired, and she turned into her cat form." Camille frowned. "And now, she won't shift back."

Shade groaned as he turned toward the living room. "You stay here—don't you go anywhere till I catch her and you turn her back." Swearing under his breath, he headed into the living room, where he saw Delilah poised on the edge of one of the coffee tables. She was eyeing the mantel over the fireplace, even though it was harvest decorations. "Delilah—stop right there. Don't you dare—Delilah!"

But she ignored him, leaping to the mantel. There wasn't room for both her and the basket of pumpkin-shaped gourds, and she managed to catch a garland as she slipped off, bringing down the basket, the garland, and everything else with it. The mantel was bare, there were decorations everywhere, and Delilah sat on the ground, looking a little dazed, with the garland around her fuzzy neck.

Shade pounced, scooping her up, and he carried the struggling tabby to the kitchen, where he plunked her down on the counter. He held her down, even though she was squirming to get free. "Change her back. Now."

Camille nodded, closing her eyes. She held out her hands.

"Two from one, to one from two,
This spell I now remove from you,
Shift now from the form we see,
As I will, so mote it be."

Amid a sputter of sparks, a faint blue light emerged to engulf Delilah. The tabby let out a brief yowl, but stopped squirming. Shade let go, jumping aside to avoid being in the way when she transformed back. A moment later, Delilah still sat there, in her cat form, her fur a bit ruffled.

"Why isn't she back to normal?" Shade glanced at Camille.

"I don't know. That should have turned her back...well...maybe."

"What do you mean *maybe*?"

She shrugged. "The spell I used on her originally was the bilocation spell. It backfired. This was a basic spell to break another spell but apparently it's not working on the bilocation spell. Another backfire." Camille picked up Delilah and held her up in the air by the belly. "You are so cute, you are so pretty—what a pretty girl!"

"Camille!" Shade stopped as she turned around, her eyes narrowed. Oops, it didn't do to yell at one of the women allowing you to live in her house. Especially since she was married to a full-blooded dragon. "I'm sorry. I'm just...what are we going to do?"

"My guess is that she'll change back when she's ready. Or the spell wears off. And it will wear off—that much I know. I just...don't know when."

Shade stared at her, his mouth open. "How long could it take?"

Camille shrugged, giving Delilah another kiss on the head. "The longest one of my backfires took to wear off—the time I made my clothes invisible—a week." Before Shade could say another word, she shoved Delilah in his arms. "We'd better get going. Don't worry—I'm sure it will wear off before the weekend's over. Just watch her closely and keep her out of trouble."

And with that, Camille darted out the door, followed by Menolly, leaving Shade alone holding his fiancée by the collar.

SHADE STARED AT the door as it slammed shut behind them. What the hell? He glanced down at Delilah, who twisted in his arms, trying to get free. The next moment, she playfully sank her claws into him and, startled, he let go. As she landed on the floor, she darted off into the laundry room.

"Delilah! Delilah, you come back here." Shade darted after her, then forced himself to stop. It wasn't like she hadn't run around in cat form enough at other times. And chances were, if he chased her, she'd stress out and that would mean it would take longer for her to transform back.

He decided to fix himself a sandwich while he waited. As he pulled out the turkey breast and bread, however, he heard a crash. "Hell, what now? They didn't forget to take Maggie with them, did they?" He raced toward the noise, following it to Hanna's room. At first he thought maybe he was right, but then he saw the playpen there, tipped over, and Delilah was struggling to drag one of the toys out of it. She loved Maggie's soft cloth balls the gargoyle played with, and apparently, she'd been determined to get one. Apparently, she'd miscalculated her jump, as well.

Shade righted the playpen, tossing of the balls into the hallway for Delilah to chase. As his girlfriend streaked out of the room, he muttered, "Damned cat," under his breath and finished tidying up the mess she'd made. Another minute, and he heard another crash from the living room. "Delilah! What the hell are you getting into now?"

As Shade made a beeline for the noise, he thought of Camille. *I hope she falls in a patch of poison ivy*. But the thought slipped away as yet another loud thud caught his attention.

TWO HOURS LATER, he had cleaned up the harvest decorations twice, swept up a broken vase, cleaned up a hairball off the sofa, and had wrestled the turkey breast away from a very determined feline. Finally, he gave up and opened the back door as Delilah howled to go outside.

"Fine, go. Play. Don't get yourself in any trouble." As she bounded out to the back porch and down the steps, he let out a disgruntled sigh. "So much for a romantic evening in front of the fire. Damn it, this is all Camille's fault." But inside, he knew it wasn't. It was as much Delilah's as her sisters. And if Delilah hadn't been torn about wanting to go up to the barrow with all of them—if he'd given in and gone with them, this wouldn't have happened and they might be taking an nice evening stroll together through the woods.

Turning back to the kitchen, he opened a can of cat food and put it down, then dashed up stairs to sift the litter box. They were in this situation together, so he'd do what he could and maybe they could salvage part of the weekend. It was still only Friday night.

A thought occurred to him, and he went out back, standing in the rain as he called for Delilah to come in. Luckily, she came racing up after a few minutes, looking wild eyed but happy. He managed to scoop her up and carry her inside. Her heart was thudding from the run, but she reached up and excitedly licked his nose, purring, and Shade couldn't help but laugh.

"Come on, Minx. Time for Jerry Springer and Cheetos." He knew the way to her heart. As he grabbed the bag of snacks off the counter and carried her into the living room where the TV was tuned into the Talk Show Channel, he hoped this would be enough to coax her back to her regular form. He settled down, trying not to grimace as the crowd began to shout, "Jerry! Jerry! Jerry!" and Delilah curled up beside him. He held out a Cheeto and she sniffed it, then bit into it, smearing her fur with the bright orange powder. It was brighter than her fur, but at least it wasn't on the few parts of her that were pale—almost white.

"You love this show, right Kitten? I don't see what's so hot about Springer, but hey, whatever floats your boat. Or squeaks your mouse, as the case may be."

She sprawled out, draping over his lap, and he softly stroked her fur, smiling gently as she purred loud enough to rival a motorboat. But, by the end of the show, she was still in cat form. Shade let out a sigh and glanced at the clock. It was only eleven, but maybe, a good night's sleep would do the trick, and he sure needed one.

"To bed, pumpkin?"

She *purped*, gazing up at him with wide emerald eyes, as he scooped her up and, making certain the house was locked, headed upstairs with her draped over his shoulder. As he settled down in bed, missing her by his side—missing her soft skin beneath his fingers, Delilah slowly padded across the covers. She crawled on his side, curled up, and promptly fell asleep.

AROUND 4:00 AM, Shade woke up. Something was wrong. Delilah wasn't in bed—in either form—and he had the sense that something was off. He slipped out from beneath the covers and put on his slippers, then pulled on his robe and tied it shut. As he reached for the light, wary and trying to listen for whatever might be setting off his internal alarm, a yowl split the silence, followed by another.

Delilah! And she sounded in pain.

Shade turned on the light, whirling to see where the cries were coming from. But then, he realized, they were echoing up the stairs. He headed toward the door on the run, trying to pinpoint where her hisses and screams were coming from.

"Delilah! Where are you? Delilah!"

Thudding down the steps, he realized that she was in the kitchen. Fuck, what had happened? Had she hurt herself? He raced into the room, slamming his hand against the light switch. As the light flared through the room, he saw Delilah, facing what looked like a mottled gray gremlin. It had wings, very bat-like, and looked a little like Maggie, except for the tiny horns on its head, and the jutting horn on its snout.

"Delilah! Get away from there—those creatures can—" Before he could catch her, she gave one final swipe at the gremlin and it swiped back at her, its claws raking her side. She let out another ear piercing shriek as faint lines of red began to dapple her fur.

"Oh no you don't!" Shade leapt forward, grappling the creature. The gremlin tried to bite him but he squeezed its throat—hard—and cleanly snapped its neck. As he dropped it, whirling to Delilah, she was huddled down, hissing and yowling. The cuts were bleeding—not swiftly, but it looked painful. Shade knew that gremlins didn't carry any venom or toxin, but he also knew that the claws were extremely sharp and he had to get Delilah to a doctor right away.

Not sure what to do first, he finally settled for grabbing her cell phone out of her pack where she'd left it, and punched in the number for the FH-CSI. Within moments, Yugi—the second in command—came on line. "Give me the medic unit, quick. This is Shade."

Yugi transferred him and, another moment and Mallen came on line. "I need your help. Delilah's been hurt."

"What happened?"

"A gremlin injured her." Shade was frantic now,

trying to keep his attention on Delilah while he talked to the healer.

The elf cleared his throat. "That shouldn't be too bad—bring her in."

"She's in cat form and it looks very painful."

"Cat form?" Another beat, and then Mallen let out a sigh. "Can you catch her? I'm dealing with several emergencies tonight, and can't get away that easily. Or you can take her to a vet—there has to be an all night clinic nearby."

"A vet. You want me to take Delilah to the vet?" Shade frowned.

Delilah perked up at the word. Her eyes narrowed and she glanced around, as if ready to bolt.

"Yes, there's an all night emergency clinic just half a mile from you—you can make it there a lot quicker than you can get here, and the wait probably won't be as long. We're fending with the aftermath of a car wreck tonight and we have four wounded Fae, two critically injured Weres and one very pissed off vampire." Mallen sounded overwhelmed. "If she's not in life-threatening danger, it would be very helpful if you could just...take her to the vet."

Shade mumbled an "Okay," and punched the END TALK button. There was a cat carrier in the laundry room—Iris had used it often enough to corral Delilah when she was causing havoc. But Shade had his doubts whether Delilah had ever been to a veterinarian's office or not. Be that as it may, it was obvious she knew what the word meant.

"Delilah, honey, you're hurt. I need to get you to

a doctor." He slowly moved toward her. She hissed and pulled away, baring her teeth. This wasn't going to be easy. "Come on, baby. Just hold still."

As he lunged forward, she sprang off the counter, still meowing, and raced out of the room, though not nearly as swiftly as she'd been running before. A trail of little droplets of blood followed her. Swearing, Shade softly followed her. He didn't want to wind her up—she could hurt herself far worse that way. But he had to catch her.

Another go round and she headed upstairs. He shifted through the Ionyc Sea to the top of the steps, but she was quick and she darted past him before he could scoop her up. She headed into the bedroom, and he followed. The next thing he knew, she had crawled under the bed.

"Delilah, come out of there." Shade glanced around, then closed the door. At least this way, she couldn't get out of the room. He closed the closet door, too, but left the door to the bathroom open. If she ran in there, she'd be easier to corner.

Dropping to his hands and knees, he leaned down and peeked under the bed. She was hunched in the center—and with a king-sized bed, that meant he couldn't reach her. He might be tall but his arms weren't that long. Neither could he fit beneath the bed.

They eyed each other for a while. Delilah let out a faint mew and it tore his heart that she was hurt and frightened to let him help. He knew that, in her state, she was probably thinking more with her cat's self, than her human-Fae side, but it still made him ache to think she didn't trust him enough to come out.

"Delilah, honey—we need to take you to the doctor. Please, come out. Please trust me. I wouldn't do this except you're hurt. Mallen said you need to be seen. We don't want those wounds infected." He spoke softy and slowly, trying to coax her out.

After a few minutes, though, it was apparent she wasn't going to budge. Shade pushed himself to a sitting position. What the hell could he use to get her out? He glanced around the room, and then saw the plant mister. He'd used it on occasion when she got too rambunctious and he wanted her to quit bugging him and get serious. Now, he picked it up and leaned over so she could see him.

"I don't want to have to use this, especially when you aren't feeling well." He shook the bottle. The water sloshed inside and Delilah let out another mew and began to back up toward the other side of the bed. As he shook it again, she popped out the other side and headed for the door. Without pausing, Shade dropped the mister and once again, shifted through the Ionyc Seas to appear right behind her. If she tried to race back under the bed, she'd have to go around him.

She darted to the left, but he was faster this time and managed to scoop her up into his arms, trying to avoid holding her where she was hurt. Delilah let out a soft cry, but then snuggled against him, giving up. Shade carried her downstairs and she reluctantly let him put her in the carrier. As they headed out into the night, he was grateful he'd gotten his license and could drive her Jeep. Otherwise it would be a cold, blustery walk in the rain.

THE VET STARED at Delilah. "Last time I saw her, she was six feet tall." The man let out a laugh and glanced over at Shade. "She brought in a couple of mice for treatment."

Shade had been relieved to find out the vet was not only aware of who Delilah was, but he was Earthside Fae—a healer by nature, if Shade guessed right.

"She's under a backfired spell and either can't— or won't—turn back. A gremlin snagged her a good one." Shade frowned. "She'll be okay, won't she, doc?"

Doctor Burberry examined her heart and then gently looked at the scratches on her side. "We'll get some salve for these so they'll heal up without infection. She's lucky—the gremlin didn't scratch terribly deep, and the fact that she's a Were makes all the difference. If she were just a regular cat? She'd probably need to be hospitalized for a few nights. But I should take her temperature." He glanced over at Shade, grinning, as he held up the thermometer.

Delilah yowled, loudly, and seconds later, her golden fur shimmered as she quickly shifted back into human form. The next moment, she had practically fallen off the table because it was made for regular size cats, not six-foot tall women.

"Welcome back." Dr. Burberry laughed. "I thought that might change matters."

Shade leaped up. "You weren't stuck?"

She blushed, then winced as she rubbed her side. "Um...no. I was...oh never mind."

"I suspect that Delilah was trying to teach you some lesson she thought you needed to learn." The veterinarian motioned for her to raise her shirt. "This salve will work on you regardless if you're a cat or not." As he slathered on the medication, the bright red slashes on her side began to fade. "There, and let that teach you not to tangle with a gremlin in your tabby-cat form. Next time, it could be worse."

As Shade led a very penitent Delilah out of the room, he contemplated yelling at her. But it wouldn't do any good, and the fact was, she'd alerted him to a gremlin who had somehow gotten through the wards. As they headed back to the car, she hesitantly reached out and took his hand.

"Forgive me? I guess...when I shifted form, I realized that I was angry because you never really asked me if I wanted to stay home. You told me we needed to, and I really wanted to go with the rest of our family." She shrugged. "I should have just said so from the beginning."

Shade forced back a sigh. As much as he liked time alone with her, this was who she was—a woman devoted to those she loved. "I know I rode over your wishes. I just...I guess I just wanted to feel like I was special in your life. Like you wanted to be with me—without needing anybody else around."

Delilah whirled around. "I love you, Shade. Always know that. I love you, and you are so very important to me. Along with my sisters, you matter the most to me. But face it, we're a package deal—all of us." She paused, then, and glanced up at the sky. The clouds were whirling, and a chill wind gusted by. "You know what? Maybe a weekend at home without the others wouldn't hurt. Maybe...maybe we do need to take it easy. Tomorrow, we could go out for breakfast and then drive out to Snoqualmie and hike around the Falls?"

Shade smiled softly. She was giving him the weekend. She was offering an olive branch, and so could he. "All right. Then, why don't we plan out a big dinner for Sunday night when the others come back. Sunday, we can go shopping for groceries, maybe see a movie, and cook? And then, when your sisters get back, we'll have a party."

She squeezed his hand and he wrapped his arm around her shoulder. "It will be a *purr-fect* weekend," she added, trilling her *r's* as she let out a soft purr and snuggled into his embrace.

Part Three

Men of Otherworld:
Collection Two

Fae-ted to Love

Sometimes, it's so wrong, it's right.

This story takes place a week or so after Panther Prowling and contains a slight spoiler for the next Camille book, but it won't ruin the book at all for you.

VANZIR TWIDDLED HIS thumbs. He glanced around, hoping that nobody noticed him, though it was a sure bet he wouldn't pass for Fae. He'd been here before, but each time, he tried to keep it as low key as possible. Aeval hadn't asked him to, but when you were boffing a Fae Queen on the side, and she hadn't broken the news to her people or her fellow nobility, it really seemed like the best idea to keep it under wraps until she made the decision. But she'd been insistent that he come out tonight, and when he pressed for a reason why, she just told him to shut up and move his ass. Maybe not in those terms, but the gist was there.

That was how he had come to be standing in a private waiting room, deep within the Barrow belonging to the Court of Shadow and Night.

Vanzir glanced around. The only other people wandering by were servants and a couple of guards, and they ignored him. He had a feeling they were trained to ignore strangers unless specifically instructed to wait on them—that was another thing about being connected to someone of royal blood. You learned how to turn a blind eye to anything that might get you in trouble if you accidentally spilled a secret.

The Barrow was closed—the ceilings were high, but he could sense the roots of the trees holding up the ceiling, and he could also tell they were in a different realm. The minute you walked through the doorway you were in the realm of the Earthside Fae, and there was a faint heartbeat—a rhythm that was constant and insistent. It played out in the blood and the brain, though he had a feeling that those who were of Fae or Elfin blood would never notice it. Vanzir was used to being in underground spaces, and he wasn't particularly claustrophobic, but when he thought about the fact that—to get out of here he'd have to run the gamut of guards wielding nasty big swords—it made him more than a little nervous.

The furnishings were nice, though. He'd hand it to Aeval for that. She had made the space seem both comfortable and ornate. Thickly padded benches offered seating, highly polished oak and walnut tables held trays of fruits and sweets, along with napkins, plates, and silverware. Vanzir considered fixing a plate, but then pushed the idea aside. He really wasn't hungry and he wasn't all that fond of sugar, and most of the food seemed highly sweetened.

Instead, he chose a bench off to one side and slumped against the wall, alternating his gaze between the door through which he had come, and a door toward the back. If she didn't come out in the next ten minutes, he was leaving, summons or not.

Throughout his life, Vanzir had been at the beck and call of entirely too many people, mostly enforced. There were times he just wanted to walk away from it all, to leave his past behind, and go somewhere and create a new life for himself.

Life had been a lot easier before he'd switched sides, at least in some ways. Back then he was a slave and he knew it. He had his place in the world, even if he hadn't liked it. Now, though, he felt like a man without a country. He was a demon fighting against demons. He was a slave set free in body, but in his mind he still remembered the agonizing days he spent in servitude to Karvanak, the Rāksasa.

After he'd turned sides, after Iris had bound him to the D'Artigo sisters, his life had still depended on the whim of others. And while they had never taken advantage of him, and never forced him into an uncomfortable situation, the fact was he had still been their property and his life was forfeit if any one of them had decided he needed to be put out of commission.

Now though, Vanzir was free. Sticking around

was his choice, but sometimes he wasn't sure why he had. True, the only place that had ever remotely felt like home was in the D'Artigo household. And true, he fully believed in the cause against Shadow Wing—the Demon Lord was the doom of everything sane that walked in the three realms, and Vanzir couldn't just walk away and ignore the threat. But sometimes...sometimes he thought about hitting the road and seeing where it took him.

A voice interrupted his thoughts. "Demon, the Queen will see you now."

The guard flashed him a disdainful sneer before leading him back to Aeval's personal meeting chamber. Essentially a private parlor, it was where she greeted guests she knew weren't going to try to assassinate her.

Vanzir had been here a good many nights over the past months. Ever since he had aided Aeval during Camille's initiation into her Priestess-hood, the Fae Queen had taken a liking to him. And, he had to admit, he enjoyed her company, and more than in the bedroom. They had a surprising amount of fun together, and a surprising amount of conversation had passed between them.

The guard dismissed herself, shutting the door behind her. A door opposite, leading to Aeval's bedchamber, opened, and out stepped the Queen of Shadow and Night in all her glory. Instead of her robes, she wore a sheer blue nightgown, and though her crown still encircled her head, her hair was long and flowing, and she had taken off her jewelry.

"Vanzir..." Her voice husky, Aeval swept forward to lock the door.

Vanzir opened his arms and she walked into them. His focus immediately narrowed to the warm, welcoming woman in his embrace. Aeval could be vicious, she could be heartless and ruthless but with him, she let her guard down. She had cried in his presence, and she had laughed—neither of which she could do in public without being aware of who was watching.

Aeval pressed against him, her breasts full and ripe beneath the gown, unfettered by bra or corset. Vanzir let out a soft moan as he slowly reached up to press his hand against her right breast, the nipple stiffening as he leaned down to take it between his lips and suck hard, giving it a little nip through the sheer material.

"What did you want?" His words were muffled by her chest, and she hooked one of her legs around the back of his own, her arms draped over his shoulders. They were about the same height, but she seemed so much taller, her power boosting her aura to tower over the room.

"You. I needed *you*. Did anyone from your home follow you?" Aeval leaned in, nipped his neck, licking the flesh then biting lightly.

He glanced up. "No, they never do. Nobody knows about us. Nobody's seen us." Each time, it was the same routine. She would fret, and he would calm her fears, and then they'd fuck so hard they'd both pass out. He wasn't complaining—there was something addictive about Aeval and he found it hard to turn away from her, but was getting tired of trying to find excuses for why he had to come out to Talamh Lonrach Oll. He had a feeling they were getting suspicious. And if Aeval was so worried about anybody finding out, then he wasn't sure how he felt about being the ghetto she was slumming in, so to speak.

As if reading his mind, she pushed him away, panting lightly. He found it hard to take his gaze off her breasts. They were magnificent, round globes that he could lose himself in. And the rest of her body was a pretty sight too. Though, he had to admit, she wasn't a demon and that was one downfall. He liked his own kind, though he wasn't averse to taking a header into bed with a number of other species and races.

She let out a long, slow breath. "How do you feel when I ask that? When I ask you if they suspect anything about us?"

He caught her gaze. Unlike the majority of other people, he wasn't afraid to look her in the face. He'd stared down far worse, and survived far harsher masters. "Like your private vibrator."

A beat...then—"That doesn't reflect well on me, does it?"

"No, but it's what you choose. How long have we been...what would you call it? *Fraternizing*?"

Arching her eyebrows, she snorted. "Point taken. We've been...*fraternizing*...since shortly after you ended up screwing Camille in the sewers. You're lucky that dragon of hers didn't toast you up and gobble you down, you know."

"Camille will be the first to tell you, that was an isolated incident. And she stopped Smoky from tearing me to pieces."

"But did you like it?" Aeval wasn't acting coy—that wasn't her nature, but he knew she was baiting him for some reason.

He shrugged. "I'd be lying if I said I didn't enjoy it. She's hot and she's sex incarnate. But I didn't set out to get in her pants, and she would never have offered herself if I hadn't been in danger of feeding on her mind. So I'd say that's a fair trade-eoff, wouldn't you? And Lizard Boy was an idiot. The price for his temper tantrum was so high that I doubt he'll ever throw another one that big. He learned the hard way what harm possessiveness can bring."

Aeval nodded. "The big lug worships her."

"Well, he almost destroyed her with his anger. It was his fault she was out in the woods. It was his fault Hyto was able to catch her so easily. And *that* dragon was one huge old ball of fun and toys. I'm just surprised Camille didn't ask for him to be flayed alive at the tribunal. I would have. She's definitely a better person than I am."

"If I had been there, he would have suffered. Trust me." Aeval shook her head, sobering. "But what is done is done, and he is dead."

Vanzir nodded. After they'd rescued her from Hyto and she was safe at home, Vanzir had invited Smoky to step out in private. In fear of his life, the demon had confronted the dragon and taken the idiot apart, dressing him down to the point where Smoky was in tears by the time they were done. They had never spoken of the meeting to anybody else, but Smoky had apologized to Vanzir and even though they maintained their surly relationship publicly, in private they were actually becoming friends.

Aeval sighed, and Vanzir opened his arms.

But Aeval shook her head and languidly stretched out on one of the benches, crossing her legs beneath the sheer panel of her gown, leaving nothing to the imagination. "You care about the family, don't you?"

Vanzir didn't really want to answer that. He wasn't comfortable admitting to emotion. But he knew Aeval, and he knew better than to try to distract her. "Yeah, I guess I fit in there. I'm a misfit among misfits."

"You're a part of their life now." She leaned forward. "You know what I've told Camille?"

He glanced over at her. "No, what?"

"You mean she hasn't said anything yet?" Aeval looked puzzled.

Vanzir cleared his throat. Sometimes the Fae Queens were out of touch with the real world, that was all he had to say on the subject.

"Aeval, we just finished shafting a psycho Viking warrior out of an ancient sword. Nobody's had much of a chance to rest up this past week. With Shade losing some of his powers, it's been even more chaotic. And I know what he is feeling, so I've been trying to be there for him."

Vanzir stared at his feet. He knew exactly what losing one's powers was like—it had happened to him. More than once he'd been tempted to take a walk with the half-dragon, to bring it out into the open and face it square on. They always said that was the first step in healing. But for one thing, there hadn't been any time to do so...not yet. And secondly—Vanzir wasn't entirely sure what to say. It was a little like going up to someone and saying, "Hey, how's it feel to have that arm cut off?" Nope, much better idea to let things settle before approaching a touchy subject. Especially a half-dragon.

"Yes, I can imagine," Aeval murmured. She let out a short, hard sigh. "I probably shouldn't tell you this because it's her news to tell."

Subterfuge and secrets. Vanzir wanted to know what she was hinting about. Knowledge meant power. But the demon also had a peculiar honor code, one he'd slowly built up over the years of abuse and humiliation spent as a sex slave. "Don't tell me."

"What?"

"Don't tell me. If it's her news to tell, then don't. I'll wait to find out till she's ready to say something." He paused. "Does it involve me?"

"Indirectly."

"But not immediately?"

Aeval shook her head. "No. Not immediately."

"Then I should wait." If there was one thing Vanzir respected, it was the right to privacy. He'd had so little of it throughout his life.

When he was born, his mother had sold him to a trader in the Sub-Realms. From the time he was barely able to walk, he'd been trained and used as a weapon. Then he was traded to a general in the demon army. There he was both weapon and pleasure boy. After that, he'd been used as a bet in a poker game and Karvanak had won him. Life had become pure hell then. The Rāksasa liked it rough and enjoyed inflicting pain. Vanzir had watched the tiger-shifting demon rape woman after man after woman, then shift and tear them to pieces for dinner when he was done.

Aeval smiled softly. "You are an interesting man, my sweet."

"I'm not a man, I'm a demon." Vanzir caressed her cheek, then flashed her a soft smile that he reserved for very few people. Aeval intrigued him. He was wary of her—she had far more power than even the girls realized—but he also respected her.

"You aren't afraid of me. I like that."

"I'm cautious...but afraid? I reserve that for the true horrors of the world."

And then, he took her in his arms. His lips pressed against hers, as she dropped her head back, gasping.

"Feel me. Touch me. Make me remember what it's like to be a woman." Aeval rested her head on his shoulder, her eyes wide.

Vanzir stared at the Fae Queen, then pulled her tight. Her hair cascaded down to her knees, the silken strands shrouding her back. She was the Queen of Night, the Queen of Shadow and Darkness, and she had walked the hidden paths of the world for thousands of years. He was holding a goddess in his arms, and he could feel the weight of the world on her shoulders. She had lived through the splitting of the worlds, had fought against the Great Divide and been frozen in crystal for her efforts. She had led armies, protected her people...and now once again she was a rising power in the world.

"Why me?" he whispered softly in her ear as he pressed his lips to her neck.

"Because you understand what it means to be trapped. You were a slave...I am a slave to my power and position. There will never be a respite for me, not until the day that I die. I carry the weight of the night on my shoulders. So many—even of my own kind—have forgotten what that means. What that entails." She stroked his face, searching his gaze. "The moon rises as it will, but I am part of the power that summons the night and shadow to the world so that it might rest. I am the silent hollows, the dust of the graveyard, the barren fields of winter, and the harsh snows that blanket the world."

Vanzir nodded. He understood—she wasn't speaking in metaphor. If the Dark Fae Queen were to die, the world would be compromised. Same thing for the light. "What happens now that Morgaine is dead? What will happen to the world of twilight and dusk?"

Aeval gazed into his eyes. "I was trying to tell you that, my sweet. Camille will be taking the post. Titania and I...along with Derisa...the Moon Mother has touched us all with the decree. Soon—on Samhain—she will undergo her initiation and we will bring her into our fold."

The news hit like a sledge hammer. Vanzir stepped back a moment, caught short by the news. "*Camille* will be one of the Fae Queens?"

"So as the Moon Mother decrees, so it will be.

We told her a week or so ago...I don't think she's confided to anyone but Delilah and Menolly yet." Aeval smiled cunningly. "She's the right choice, and will be a far better queen than her cousin was."

"I never realized she aspired to power such as this..." Vanzir frowned. The Camille he knew would be terrified by the news. But she hadn't seemed any different to him. Then again, he hadn't really been paying attention.

"She doesn't, and that is precisely why she makes such a good choice. She will also be an excellent bridge between the human side of affairs and the world of the Fae. Times are changing and we must adapt. The world can never go back to what it was. The Merlin will be returning to our shores for the initiation, and we believe he means to stay here."

Aeval turned to him. "And this brings me to you. You must make a choice. Once her initiation is complete, she and her husbands will be moving to the Barrow of Dusk and Twilight. You will have the choice whether to stay with her sisters, or to join us here, as my official consort. You will wield no power over the Sovereign Nation, but you will be accorded all the respect that the position is due."

And the explosions just kept on coming. Vanzir thought he was immune to surprise but the past few minutes had proven him wrong. He gently let go of Aeval and, shaking, took a seat near her. "You want me to come out as your lover? To officially announce that I'm your consort?"

"We've been together for some time. I am tired of hiding my lover." Aeval winked at him. "Nobody is going to counter my choice—they're too afraid of me."

"But...surely they'll expect you to choose from the men here—" Vanzir trailed off. If Aeval had wanted a lover from the men of Talamh Lonrach Oll, she would have chosen one already. She wanted him, and she was willing to tell the world he was hers.

She shook her head. "They expect me to choose the lover I want. If they object, you will never hear it in your presence. Far too dangerous for dissidents."

Pausing, she tilted her head to the side. "I don't think you understand yet. As worldly and jaded as you are, I truly don't believe you understand the scope of my power. Add in this bit of information: The war against Shadow Wing is closer than you think. All my seers predict it. If we win it, the world will forever change."

"We?"

"*We.* The Fae will stand alongside the D'Artigo sisters and the dragons and the daemons. Humans will realize the demons exist. The governments will have to learn they are far less powerful than they think. Their biggest and most nightmarish weapons only strengthen the creatures. Anything radioactive is basically a steroid shot for the damned demons. The dragons will be outing themselves, and the mortals will see that they exist. After the war, the human world...won't be so human-centric."

She paused. "Surely, you've thought about what it will be like."

Vanzir shook his head, speechless. Truth was,

he hadn't. He had always assumed that the war would be fought out of sight, out of the reach of humankind, but what she said made sense. Unless they took the fight directly into the Sub-Realms, mortals were going to get an eyeful and realize that the Fae and vamps and Weres were only the tip of the iceberg.

"Yes...you begin to see now." Aeval trailed a finger along his shoulder, the silk of her gown shifting with a gentle hush as she moved to stand beside him. He found himself staring through the sheer material directly at her torso, and at the soft V where her thighs met. His body responded, his cock rising hard and insistent.

"Fuck me." Her voice was throaty, with a trill of laughter behind it.

Vanzir took her hand in his. It was delicate and small, so unlike the nature of her power. As he raised her fingers and kissed them one by one, pressing his lips to each pale tip.

Aeval let out a short, harsh breath, then inhaled deeply, her breasts rising full as she shuddered. Vanzir slid his hand beneath her gown and trailed his palm up the outside of her thigh, rounding over the curve of her hip. She moaned gently and slowly spread her legs, just enough to make him harder than ever. The dark thatch of hair shimmered against the slight rise of her mound, curly and promising every hidden secret he could think of.

"Will you?" Her voice was husky. She stopped back, pulling away to stare down at him with a haughty, teasing smile. "Will you come out and live with me, and join me as my love? Will you learn what it's like to be consort to the Queen of Shadow and Night?"

Vanzir stood, stripping off his T-shirt. He began to back her up toward the door leading into her bedroom. "I already *am* your consort. But yes, I will come and live with you and be your lover, as long as you never try to control me."

"There will be rules—there are always rules." Aeval backed away, light on her feet, a gleam flickering in her eye. "You know that if you are with me, there will never be total freedom. But you will always be free to leave. I will never stop you if you want to go. Not even now. Not even if you turn away from me at this moment. I will never enslave you or bewitch you." She was pressed up against the wooden door, her eyes glittering.

With a rough laugh, Vanzir reached around behind her and opened the door. "You already have bewitched me, my brilliant star in the dark of night." He walked her backwards into the bed chamber.

The huge bed was carved from elder and yew, ancient and dark wood rising up on all four sides— the posters held a canopy draped in black and silver silk curtains. The comforter was also black and silver, shimmering as if a thousand stars had been dusted across it. The room held dressers and wardrobes, a vanity and a private bath, and everything a queen could need including a small desk to one side. But right now, Vanzir's focus was the bed itself.

Vanzir dropped his shirt on the floor, then reached down and slowly began to unbuckle his jeans. His chest glistened in the dim light. He was wiry but toned, his waist lean. He slid his jeans down to reveal a tight, round ass and muscled thighs. Erect, thick and meaty, his cock was ready for action, with drops of pre-cum glistening on the tip. With a low growl, he grasped his shaft and squeezed as he stared at Aeval, a light flashing in his eyes which whirled with a vortex of indescribable colors.

Aeval caught her breath, and reached up to unhook the top of her gown. It fell open, like a robe. She shrugged it off, standing there in her pale, unearthly beauty. Her breasts were firm and ripe, and her waist curved into soft, voluptuous hips, lush and inviting. Vanzir felt the hunger within him rise, and he fought down the desire to feed on her mind. With Aeval, though, he knew the danger was miniscule. The Fae Queen could fight him off. She could kill him if the dream-chaser demon within him went amok. Vanzir didn't have to hold himself back with her.

"You know what I need," she whispered, trailing her fingers over the full, dark nipples that marked her breasts. "You know what I need," she repeated.

He nodded, and leapt forward, grabbing her wrists and throwing her down to the bed. She laughed, roughly, as he landed on top of her, thrusting her knees apart with his own. Aeval wasn't a gentle lover and neither was he. When they played, they played hard. As hard as rocks in a river, as hard as the erection that was driving him forward.

Pressing against her, he trailed love bites up and

down her chest, nipping lightly—not enough to hurt but enough to make her know he had hold of her. She gasped again, wrapping her legs around his waist and thrusting upward, rubbing against his cock.

"Not yet, not yet..."

"Yes...now. I need you *now*. I don't want gentle. We can do gentle later. Fuck me, fuck me hard." She let out a growl.

And so, he drove into her, spreading her pussy wide as he grunted, thrusting into the darkness of her sex. She moaned, tightening the embrace of her knees around his waist, pulling him deeper into her wet slit.

As he plunged into her, driving himself again and again, Aeval began to whimper, and then she squirmed. He reached down to finger her, laughing low as she let out first one shriek, then another. She was coming hard, coming fast, and in some small part of his brain, Vanzir realized something must have happened to trigger off the need. She usually liked to take her time, to luxuriate in their foreplay and slowly spread it out for hours. But today she was frantic in her hunger, and his own desire rose to match her need.

He speared himself into her again as she climaxed yet again. The passion in her voice, the feeling of her channel clenching him damp and tight drove him over the edge. His back arching, Vanzir dropped his head back and let out a low, long growl as he came, the spasm ricocheting through his body. Collapsing between her legs, he let out a muffled moan. Then, slowly, he reached up to kiss her on the nose, the tousled shock of platinum hair mixing with her own dark locks.

"That was quick, love." He rolled to one side and took her in his arms, snuggling her close to him. "Are you sure you're satisfied? Do you want more?"

She sighed, reaching for the comforter and pulling it over them. "I'm good for now." A pause, then—"There's a lot on my mind right now. Ever since Morgaine died, I've been caught up in a whirlwind of what-if's. The world has changed so much. And, while I know we have to adapt, I feel rather lost and alone. Titania is coping better than I am—I think it's because the light has an inherent nature to look to the bright side of things." She sat up, settling against the pillows that cushioned the headboard. "The world has grown much smaller. I feel hemmed in."

"Yet, you would never consider moving to Otherworld?" Vanzir wrapped his arm around her. She needed him to listen and so he leaned her against his shoulder and kissed the top of her head.

"I fought against the creation of Otherworld. You cannot begin to understand what horrors the Great Divide brought about. This world was rocked by the fighting. The earthquakes...volcanoes erupting...our magic almost destroyed what civilization there was. Sometimes, I think it would have been best if that had happened, given the way the world is now."

"But you lost." Simply said, and plainly meant.

She understood and nodded. "Yes, we lost. The Great Fae Lords won and the rest is history. Perhaps if *we* had won, if the worlds had remained united, then there would be more respect for nature. Or, perhaps the demons would have demolished everything long ago and made it into a wasteland. Your kind, my love—not *you* in particular, but demons—aren't exactly known for your love of the wilderness."

Vanzir had to agree there. "As much as it pains me to say this, the Great Divide did the world a service far more than an injustice. It was catastrophic, but it sealed off the Sub-Realms."

"Yet it was a solution with a time limit. The portals can't hold much longer. We're seeing them break down as the months go by. The mages are looking for solutions. The elves were close until Telazhar destroyed Elqaneve. Now, all their research is in the dust. We've been searching for survivors—for the techno-mages who might have lived. We've sent search parties, but so few survived. I fear the Elfin race will take millennia to recover."

She pushed her way out of bed to pace around the room. Finally, she turned to him. "I'm afraid the old ways are gone. No matter what, change is upon us and..." She paused, raising her hand to her stomach. "Change has come to me."

"What do you mean?" Vanzir rose, sitting on his knees on the bed. He had the feeling that an arrow was coming right down the center of the room and he was right at the center of its aim.

"Vanzir...I'm pregnant."

Silence. Her words reverberated through the room, finally making a beeline for Vanzir's skull, where he suddenly realized *what* she had said. "How...how can..."

"You know most demons can interbreed with humans. Apparently, it works with Fae too. At least, we've established that now. I have had no other lover for so long that...I can't remember when the last one caught my eye. Before I was frozen in the caves." She turned to him. "I had no idea this could happen. I'm talking to the healer tomorrow to see if she thinks it dangerous for me to carry the child to term. Or if...it even has a chance. But I felt you should know, regardless of what happens or what I choose to do."

The world fell very silent. Vanzir dropped back on the bed, staring at her. *Pregnant.* He had actually gotten someone pregnant, and a Fae Queen at that. In all his years, he had never once had a woman tell him this—demon or otherwise. And the truth was, he wasn't sure how to respond, or even how he felt.

"I never thought this could happen."

"Neither did I, but the horses are out and it's too late to close the barn door." She caught his gaze, holding it lightly. "I'm not going to ask how you feel. This sort of news goes down best with a drink and some time to think. Nor am I going to tell you what I plan on doing yet...I need more information. But if it is safe for me to have the child and I decide to do so, I'd like her...him...to know that you are the father."

No wonder she was asking him to move in.

"And if it's not safe...if things don't work out?" Vanzir tilted his head to the side. "Do you still want me?" He realized, with a sudden pang in his heart, that he very much wanted her to say yes. He also realized that the fact that her answer mattered, scared the hell out of him.

She smiled softly. "If I didn't want you, I wouldn't ask you to be my consort. I wouldn't tell you about this child. I'd quietly do what I needed to, and that would be it. No, Vanzir, whatever fortune brought us together, whatever the Hags of Fate have planned, there's something about you that I…" She paused.

He could hear the word hovering between them. "You don't have to say it—not yet. Our lives move slowly. I don't need to hear it right now and I'm not sure if I can say it back to you. Not yet. But I care about you. I want you, Aeval. I want to be with you and hold you in my arms and know that you're there."

Aeval padded back across the chill floor of the barrow, her breasts bouncing lightly. "Now, do you see why I needed you so much? I couldn't breathe. I couldn't imagine what you were going to say. If you walked away, my life would feel very empty again."

He held out his arms and she slid into them, shivering. Vanzir pulled the covers over them and he laid her down, leaning on his side to stare into her eyes.

"You're with a demon, you know."

She nodded, and her cunning smile was back. "Oh, I know. I'm with a demon. You're with a Fae Queen. Not exactly the star-crossed match meant to be, I would think. And yet, here we are."

Vanzir laughed. "Here we are, and you're pregnant." At that moment, he realized he hoped the baby would be safe and well. The child would never inherit the throne, but that didn't matter. The only thing that mattered was that—if all was safe—the baby would be born into a caring family and never, ever face what he had gone through. He would make certain of that.

"Well, we'll see what happens." She slid her arms around his chest, pressing against his warm, welcoming skin. "Make love to me. Softly this time...softly—for the first time."

And so, he pressed his lips to her, and the fire faded into a gentle, steady ember, but the glow was enough. It was deeply rooted, and the flames would flare again. And perhaps, a spark would rise between them, a spark that would take hold and grow strong and as darkly beautiful as the wild night. But for now, Vanzir pushed away thoughts of the future as he took his dark queen again, forgetting about everything that stood outside the barrow walls.

Smoke and Mirrors

There was a time, when Smoky first had to decide how he felt about mortal kind. This is that story. This takes place long before the D'Artigo sisters were even born.

HE SAT ON the mountain top, staring down over the rocky world below. The air was so thin that if he had been human, he would have died. But dragons were able to breathe the air at the top of the world, and Iampaatar was a prince among dragons. At least, that's what he would have been called in human society. Among his own kind, he was nobility, but he ignored that most of the time. He preferred to wander the rocky crags alone. Much to the dismay of his family, politics held little interest for him, and neither did the intricate relationships that marked the interactions among the Court.

Dragons were hierarchical. The race ran on blood and lineage, and everything about family background mattered. Iampaatar was at the top of the food chain, draconically speaking. His mother was a silver dragon—the topmost rank. She was close enough to have the Emperor's ear, and because of her blood, Iampaatar was in the highest class. But none of that mattered to him.

He leaned over the outcropping, his massive body shifting against the rocks as he adjusted his tail, wrapping it around a tall pillar of stone to keep himself balanced. His stomach rumbled and he realized that he was hungry—it had been some time since he'd eaten in his natural form. With a lazy sigh, he snorted and smoke rose from his nostrils. Stretching his wings wide, he rose up and prepared for flight. The taut, scaled wings were strong, as were all dragon wings, but he used them more for steering than anything else. They caught the updrafts and currents, but they were not the prime force that kept him aloft.

With a flickering thought that he'd rather sit and muse than go hunting, he leaned forward and swept off the crag, spiraling to the fields below.

Iampaatar circled over the forest. He usually didn't encroach into the Northlands but pickings were slim at this time of year. Winter was harsh, and farmers kept their cattle indoors rather than allow them to wander and graze.

Of course, Iampaatar could always raze a farm or house and steal whatever they had—there were few who could defend against him—but he prided himself that he wasn't like his father. He wasn't like a lot of the dragons he knew, actually.

Iampaatar would never admit it, but the truth was, he had a conscience and that was one of the major reasons he kept himself away from his mother's dreyerie as much as he did. Hyto, his father, was a monster, and they had come to blows more than once, with Iampaatar bearing the brunt of the white dragon's anger.

Hyto made him sick to his stomach with his rampaging nature. They had come to blows several times before his mother interrupted, forcing both of them to back down. This last time, she had threatened them both with expulsion, and since she was dominant rank, she could shove whoever she wanted out of the dreyerie. But Iampaatar didn't trust his father not to sneak back in and try to hurt his mother. In fact, he suspected Hyto was behind the death of several of his brothers and sisters. The white dragon was vicious and jealous, and his avaricious nature exceeded any grasp of family love or tenderness. So Iampaatar tried to restrain himself, so he could keep an eye on things.

As he silently glided over the snowscape, he realized there was a figure below, struggling through the snow. Squinting, he swept lower to see what it was. Maybe a cow or horse or some other bite that would make a crunchy meal? But as he homed in on the figure, he realized it was a human. A girl.

Hmm...what was she doing so far out from the nearest village? And what was she doing traveling alone in this weather? Another storm was coming in, and it would be upon the land before nightfall. He wondered if she knew the weather was changing. What could be so compelling to expose her to the dangers of the forest and weather without any protection or guardians?

At first, he tried to talk himself into flying away. She was none of his concern. But then, he realized it had been weeks since he had talked to another soul. Curiosity won out. He flew away before she could see him, landing in a nearby grove where he shifted into his human form. His scales and hide took the appearance of a milk-white long white robe. His hair, calf-length, shimmered like spun silver, and his eyes were pale blue with pools of frost in them. All in all, Iampaatar was a gorgeous hunk of manflesh, and he knew it.

KATJA LEANED AGAINST a tree. She was tired, so tired. The hunger in her belly burned, and her head was foggy from the lack of food. She stared up at the sky, where the clouds were gathering together again for yet another round of snow. Katja was near the top of the world and she knew it. The Northlands were harsh and rough, kissing the edge of the Dragon Reaches. There, the snow grew harsher, from difficult going to impossible to navigate. Few humans managed to breach the entrance into the Dragon Reaches, and she wasn't interested in trying.

The girl, who was barely a woman, adjusted her cloak, tightening it around her shoulders. She shivered, freezing even though beneath the heavy woolen garment she was wearing yet another robe, and then a pair of spidersilk trousers and tunic.

Winter was rough this year and the snows wouldn't stop. The food had run out, and she couldn't feed her family, so it was hunt or die by starvation. If her mother and father were alive, they'd manage—they had been excellent hunters. But her parents had been taken by wolves during the early spring, and Katja was left to fend for her brothers and sisters.

Just past her sixteenth year, by all rights she should be married with children of her own, but she couldn't just let her siblings starve. She loved them too much, and most men didn't want a ready-made family of hungry mouths. So she had done her best. She had tilled the garden, learned how to protect and heal with the magic the local midwife had taught her, hunted during the autumn migration, and done her best to fill the larders before winter caught up with them.

But now the cupboards were empty and the children were hungry, and there wasn't enough game near the house to restock. The root cellar had contained supplies she had put up during the summer—hard won and even harder kept. But a roving band of vagrants threatened to steal away her younger sisters unless Katja let them take the food. She had caved, turning over the food, and the bandits had left, thankfully, honoring their word. But they hadn't left so much as a crumb behind.

So she had no choice. Katja had to go hunting. She left Pieter, her oldest brother who was twelve now, in charge with strict instructions to bar the door against anyone they didn't know. Packing the last of the apples she could find into her pockets, Katja had set out, bow and arrows slung over one shoulder and skinning knife in her belt. She hated taking the last of the food, but she knew she would need her strength for the hunt.

That had been two days ago. Katja had managed to catch one rabbit, but that wouldn't be enough for eight hungry bellies, so she buried it in a spot she would remember, deep in the snow where the cold would preserve it, and continued on. It occurred to her that, should she find a moose or reindeer or elk, she would have no way of dragging it home, but she decided to cross that bridge when she came to it. If nothing else, she could hack as much as she could drag off of it and bury the rest, marking where it was so she could come back for it.

Meanwhile, her focus was on staying alive through the coming storm long enough to find quarry, and then staying alive long enough to kill her prey.

Katja huddled near the tree, out of the worst of the wind. Maybe she should just roll out her bed-roll and hunker in to rest for a while. As she debated the wisdom of losing more time and energy by sleeping, a sound startled her.

Turning, she caught a glimpse of something moving behind a nearby stand of fir. Silently, she slid her bow off her shoulder and brought an arrow to bear in the general direction of the noise, pausing as she waited for whatever it was to show itself. She had learned patience from her mother, who was a brilliant shot, and she had learned how to skin the animals from her father. Together, they had made an unbeatable team—that is, until the wolves had brought them down.

The sounds coming from the copse weren't those of an animal. No snuffling or growling, no sound of trampling either. Katja waited, her arrow still nocked and ready to fire. As she tried to follow the sound, gauging its proximity to her, a sudden hush fell over the area. It was as if a thousand tiny sounds suddenly stopped and the only thing she could hear was the sudden fall of snow as the storm began in earnest.

A soft flurry of snowflakes spiraled around her and she blinked, trying to see through the sudden whirl. When the gust died down, she realized that a tall man in a long white robe was standing in front of her. Silver hair flowed down his back. He was beautiful—pale as the snow itself. And his gaze was locked directly on her.

She faltered, slowly lowering the arrow, though keeping it in hand just in case. He was no bandit, though, not by the looks of him, and the robe seemed thin and light. So either he was a spirit of the cold, or he was unaffected by the weather.

"Who are you? Identify yourself." Katja kept her voice even. She'd had to learn to force the fear back—it threw opponents off guard and helped her keep her mind clear.

But he made no move to attack her. Instead, he leaned against a nearby boulder, and his hair swirled up to coil around his shoulders. She suddenly froze, then lowered the arrow. Only one creature had hair that could move like this.

Dragon.

The fear rose up again, this time so far beyond her ability to control it that she stumbled back, dropping her bow and arrow. She lost her balance and went tripping back to land butt-first in the heavy, wet snow.

The dragon began to slowly walk toward her. He didn't look in a hurry, though, and he carried no weapon. Maybe there was some way she could get out of this alive.

The next moment, he was standing over her, staring down at her prone figure. She curled into a ball, trying to protect herself. Dragons weren't above eating people. They were dangerous and fearsome and nothing she could do would make a dent. Even if she stabbed him with her skinning knife, the blade would only nick him lightly—if at all.

To fight a dragon...took an army.

As he leaned down, Katja whispered a prayer to the goddess of the hearth. *Please, let my sisters and brothers be safe. Let someone take them in and keep them alive and healthy.*

"Woman, sit up."

She forced herself to obey, waiting for whatever torment he might inflict on her. She was deter-mined to meet her death the way her people had taught her—with courage and strength.

"What's your name?"

The question caught her off guard. Dragons didn't usually talk to humans. She blinked, not certain what to do.

"Do you understand me? Can you speak, girl?" His voice was gruff, but with no underlying threat behind it.

Katja cleared her throat, stuttering as fear infected her words. "I'm...I'm Katja. Please...are you going to kill me?"

THE LOOK ON the girl's face was one of absolute terror. Iampaatar frowned. While he was used to intimidating other creatures, something about her fear unsettled him. In fact, seeing her cower back in the snows didn't suit his fancy at all. She looked petrified. Petrified and...*exhausted*. Her clothes were threadbare, if neat. Her bow and arrows looked worn, but well maintained. She couldn't be very old—at least not in human terms. All in all, she was as much of a threat to him as a gnat was.

"What are you doing out here in the woods alone, Katja? Dangers lurk everywhere. There are wolf packs running wild, and bandits, and avalanches waiting to bury the unwary." He took her hand and drew her to her feet. The wonderment that spread over her face amused him.

She curtseyed. "Lord...Dragon..."

"So you know what I am?"

"Yes, milord. Your hair betrays your nature."

He smiled faintly. "What are you doing out here?"

"Hunting for game. My brothers and sisters are

hungry, and thieves took all the food I managed to put up this summer. They'll starve if I don't find some meat to take home. They're young, milord. They need me to protect and fend for them." The words came out in a breathless rush, and as she glanced up at him nervously—she was very short and Iampaatar was six-foot-four—a rosy blush hit her cheeks.

She was comely, he'd give her that. And brave, if she was out hunting alone. "What about your parents? Why isn't your father out here?" While Iampaatar had no quarrel with women hunting or fighting, it did rankle him that her family sent her out alone. That was as good as a death sentence.

She ducked her head, the blush on her cheeks dying down. "They died early last year. A wolf pack tore them to pieces. I was there, and I only managed to escape because my mother sacrificed herself. Da had stepped in to protect us, and they caught him. The curs were after me, but Ma threw herself between us. She screamed for me to run. There was nothing I could do to help, so I ran and managed to make it back to the house. It was the end of the winter, and we had been out looking to the fields to see if the soil could be tilled yet to plant barbury roots and high corn."

"How many brothers and sisters do you have, Katja?" His voice was softer now. The matter of fact way that she told her story hit him squarely in the heart. The girl had seen her parents killed and she had taken up as best as she could, which was more than many a man would do. It was more than he expected his father would ever do.

"Three brothers, four sisters. Pieter, the oldest, is twelve. I've been teaching him to hunt, but the game near the house is scarce and winter has been long this year. I would move us into the village but we've no money for that, and I've no skills to earn our keep other than hunting and tending the garden. And I think it's healthier if they grow up in the countryside. The soot from town fires weakens the lungs." Her voice cracked.

As he gazed down at her, she looked up, pleading. He recognized the look. She was begging him not to kill her, because doing so would effectively destroy her brothers and sisters.

That, right there, made up his mind. Thinking of his own siblings, and the fact that he suspected his father of filicide—several times over—the sight of this slip of a girl trying to protect her brothers and sisters and play both mother and father to them touched him in a way that nothing else had for a long time.

"Come, then. If you need food, we'll find you food. What have you eaten today?" He looked her up and down. She was too thin and gaunt.

"I had an apple. That's all we had left." She was staring at him like he'd grown another head. "What do you mean...*we*? You're going to help me?" The disbelief in her voice both irritated and amused him. Nobody *ever* believed dragons could be helpful.

"I mean just that. Come then, I want you to close your eyes. I promise, you won't be hurt." He pulled her close. Her heart was beating like a drum afire and he knew she was terrified. As he brought his hair up to wrap around her shoulders, she gazed up at him and—whether from hunger or fear—fainted.

That makes things easier, he thought with a faint smile. Without another word, he lifted her into his arms and with a soft sound like snow falling on snow, vanished into the Ionyc Seas.

"WHAT DO YOU expect to do with her? Are you mad, son? You know what will happen should your father find her here. You know what he's like around humans." Vishana stared at her son. Iampaatar could be a handful, but at least he was always open about his intentions. But now—bringing a human into the dreyerie?

At least Hyto was out, no doubt down in his caverns toasting some poor girl over a spit after he had used her for his pleasure. Vishana had recently been toying with the idea of denying him. Divorce in the Dragon Reaches was almost unheard of—there had to be good reason to deny a spouse, and killing humans didn't play into it. Now, killing offspring...That was another matter. But she couldn't prove that her husband had been behind the deaths of their children. Until recently Iampaatar had been one of the younger sons. Now that most of his brothers were dead, he was the oldest. He was the ninth son of a ninth son—and that made him special.

Iampaatar shook his head. "I don't plan on keeping her here, Mother. But she's *starving*, and so is her family. I couldn't think of where to take her in order to get food."

"What about her village?"

"I can't very well walk into the inns in Ryddinton, can I? They'd mark me as quickly as she did, and there are some talented swordsmen there who would love to build their armor from the hide of a dragon." Iampaatar frowned. "I know it wasn't the wisest thing to bring the girl here, but I had no other choice. I'll gather enough food to see them through the winter, and take her home."

Vishana stared at her son. He was her shining hope, and though she didn't let him see it, right now she was terribly proud of him. "You are fond of her. You've always had a soft spot for the mortals, haven't you? You're as fascinated and fond of their culture as your father is disgusted by it. Very well, do what you will with her. But remember, my son," she touched his arm lightly with her hand, "You are engaged to Harasha. The day will come when you must do your duty, marry her, and take up your responsibilities here. She is a gold dragon. She is worthy enough to join our clan. And you are my son. The Council will be waiting for you to take your rightful place when you've gotten your wanderlust out of your system."

Iampaatar glanced around the chamber. It was regal, and brilliant. Looming over everything was his mother's coat of arms. The splendor that marked the status of his family was to be found in every trinket, in every stitch of cloth. He did love this place. His mother's dreyerie was beautiful and magnificent and...*home*. But it was home to a maniac, as well.

"I cannot live here. Not while my father does. Mark my words, Mother. He will destroy all of your children. He cannot stand to think they are accorded higher status than he is. He cannot face that they will inherit your wealth instead of him. His envy will taint us all someday. Get rid of him while you still live, or he may decide that you should meet with a fatal accident."

Speaking to his mother like this gave him no pleasure, but he was out of patience.

Vishana said nothing for a moment. Then, very softly—"I will consider your advice, my son. Meanwhile, take your pet, and take as much food as you like, and a bit of gold if you want, and return her to her home. Don't let your father know, because—"

"You don't need to finish the thought. I know what he'd do. He'll never know she exists." And with that, Iampaatar took his leave.

KATJA WOKE TO find herself in a strange room. Lush and opulent, it smelled like roses and jasmine, like geraniums and fresh mint. A maid, who she immediately pegged as *dragon*, silently motioned for her to undress and step into a tub of steaming water. Cowed, afraid to say no, Katja did as she was told.

Soothing herbs had been steeped in the water, and soap bubbles glided along the surface. Still in shock, she softly leaned back and closed her eyes, luxuriating in the warmth. As the water eased her muscles, the maid brought over a tray. On the tray was bread and meat, cheeses and even fruits and sweets. Her stomach aching from a gnawing hunger, it was all Katja could do to force herself to eat small bites. If she stuffed herself, her body would rebel and she would throw up. After the bath, she was given clean, heavy clothing that kept out the chill. She continued to eat, small but steady nibbling. No one came to speak to her, no one said a word. Tired and worried about her brothers and sisters, Katja finally curled up on a fur-covered bed, and within moments, she was asleep, her dreams quiet and clear as she rested.

WHEN SHE WOKE again, she was on the edge of the forest, near her house. The dragon was with her, and so was a sledge filled with bundles and bags. A full grown reindeer lay across the sledge, cleaned and gutted. Katja glanced around wildly, trying to figure out whether she had dreamed being in the fortress at the top of the world, or whether it had been real.

"What is this?" She looked up at her companion, realizing she still didn't know his name. "Who are you? What's your name?"

He grinned at her. "Dragons never give their names, surely you know that. But you may call me…" As he paused, he hiccupped and a puff of smoke appeared. He snorted as she stumbled back. "That happens. Don't let it startle you."

"Smoky...I'll call you Smoky." Katja smiled then, suddenly feeling relaxed. He was a dragon, but he hadn't killed her. She was dressed in clothing that kept the chill at bay. Her stomach was full and she had slept deep in safety. That made for a good day.

Arching one eyebrow, Iampaatar shrugged. "As you like. I've never been called that before but it will do. I've stores here, for you and your family. There's food to last you through the winter, and weapons, and clothes for your brothers and sisters. I'll put in a store of wood for you, and here...keep this hidden and don't let anybody know where you put it." He pressed ten silver coins—a small fortune for one of her status—into her hand.

Katja stared at the money. "What do I have to do to earn this?" A thought crossed her mind. She'd heard of some dragons who took women for mistresses. The thought didn't necessarily displease her, but she wanted to know the terms of his friendliness before she agreed to take anything. Better to starve a beggar than die a serf.

Iampaatar heard the question behind the question. He lifted her hand and gently kissed the top of it. "Nothing, Lady Katja. You are in need. I can give help. It pleases me to know that your family will not starve. You've shown yourself brave and loyal, and I respect that."

And with that, he guided the sledge over to the door, which burst open as a passel of children converged on her. She hugged them one by one as Pieter began to unpack the sledge. As she turned to introduce Smoky, to her surprise, he had vanished as quickly as he had appeared. She glanced into the sky. Faintly, near the treeline, she saw a speck of white winging away, and she wondered if she'd ever see him again.

TIME WENT ON. Her brothers and sisters grew, and oddly enough, no other bandits ever made their way to the door. Every few months, Katja would go out hunting, but in addition, each season there was always an an elk, or reindeer or other animal left near the house, cleaned and carved into pieces for easy carrying to the smokehouse.

Now and then, there would be a bushel of apples, or a bag of clothing. One day, she took her siblings into town to buy them new shoes and a few supplies like grain and honey, and when they returned, the house had been mended. Everything that had been broken had been fixed, and new blankets covered the beds, and a new cooking pot had replaced the old one which had sprung a leak. The village assumed she was working herself to the bone in order to take care of her brothers and sisters, and finally the headmaster of the school offered them free lessons. So she sent them to school each day, except for Pieter, who did not want to go.

Another winter passed, and another, and each time, there was food to spare, and supplies when they most needed them. Katja grew strong and beautiful, though she resisted any attempts by the men of the village to court her. Instead, she kept her gaze trained on the skies, always watching for a sign that Smoky might be returning. But she always managed to miss him, and so she spent her days wandering the woods, learning the way of the herbs and plants, listening to them and learning their speech and how to use them for healing.

Another three years out, and yet another three, and she had become the wortcunning woman for the village. By then, everybody knew her family was receiving some sort of help, but she never spoke of it, and a protective aura lingered around their cabin. No one said a word against her or her family and they became respected in the village. By then, Katja was twenty-five, and her sisters were of marrying age. She arranged good matches for them with village lads, and warned that if they were mistreated, she would send her spirits to harm them. Her brothers left home one by one to find their fortunes. One moved into the village and took up smithery. Pieter stayed by his sister's side, though.

One day they were down by the creek, talking.

"Where is the dragon?" He glanced at her, smiling. The usual stores for the winter had arrived a fortnight ago.

"What dragon?" She stared at Pieter, startled. In all these years, she had never once mentioned Smoky's name, or her adventure in the woods. She had kept her secrets, hiding them away like she hid away the silver coins that arrived with the supplies. There was a tidy store hidden in the floor of the cabin by now.

"The dragon who rescued you. I'm not stupid, Katja. I figured out several years back. Oh hell, I *saw* him. All right? I saw him bring the supplies one year. I was up early, visiting the outhouse, when he appeared with the sledge. I can tell a dragon when I see one." He leaned back, staring as the lazy leaves began to tumble down in a sudden gust of wind. Autumn was rolling in, and the snows were close behind.

Katja then, for the first time, told Pieter about her desperate hunting trip, and what had happened. "I've never seen him since then, though I'd like to."

Pieter glanced down at his older sister. He'd grown to be a tall, burly man. "You should marry, Katja. You should marry someone and be happy and make babies of your own."

But she just shook her head. How could she tell him that her heart belonged at the top of the world? That it belonged to a man she had met once, who had saved her life?

EVENTUALLY, AS THE years wore on, Pieter took a wife and moved to his own cabin. He made sure to help his sister though, and Katja became close friends with Marta and she was goddess-mother to their children. And each year, she still found her supplies waiting for her. Each year, around the time they were to arrive, she would wait and keep watch, and do her best to catch a glimpse of the tall, handsome dragon, but he always managed to evade her.

One year, she found a jeweled bracelet among the bags on the sledge. Another year, a silk gown. She had no place to wear them, but kept them neatly tucked away in the closet. The protective spell surrounding her cabin held, and her skill with herbs and wortcunning grew to the point where people came from miles around for her help. Many a man tried to win her heart, but she turned them all away.

The years passed, and then, one morning, she looked in the mirror and realized life was quickly ticking away. She touched the wrinkles on her face. Her nieces and nephews were grown with families of their own, and even their children were grown. Though Katja had kept in good health, she felt something shifting inside, and—without having to see a doctor—knew that a growth had taken root in her belly. She had seen it often enough, and though there wasn't much to be done, she knew how to make herself comfortable for however long she might have.

One evening, as the days were waning into autumn again, she was sitting outside thinking about her life when a noise in the copse startled her. She adjusted her shawl and straightened her back, waiting, her bow and arrow nearby. She was still the best shot around.

A tall man stepped from out of the tall trees, and she recognized him instantly. She stood, her back creaking and her knees popped, but her heart still felt as young as the day she had first seen his face.

"Smoky!" She broke into a wide smile as he strode over to her side.

The look on his face was tender and gentle as he knelt beside her. "Sit, Katja. Don't strain yourself." He reached out, stroked her face softly. "How are you this autumn?"

She shook her head. "I'm old, my friend. Old and growing tired. But I'm happy." As she held his gaze, falling deeply into those glacial blue eyes, she ducked her head, then smiled back. "I missed you. I wish...why did you never show yourself? I can't begin to thank you for all you've done for me and my family."

"Your gratitude spoke for itself in the way you've lived your life." He sat beside her, wrapping one strong arm around her shoulders. "My lovely Katja—hush, you *are* lovely. Age is an illusion. What matters is the heart. I didn't come to see you because I couldn't risk your life. You do not know the politics in my family, but the fact is that my father would have found you and killed you if he'd known about you. I would not compromise you nor your brothers or sisters. But I never forgot about you. I always kept watch—"

"I know. We felt your presence." Katja considered his words. They had the ring of truth. Dragons could charm, but why would he bother lying to an old woman? She inhaled deeply, then slowly let her breath whistle out, all the hopes and wishes of her youth vanishing with it, leaving behind a soft contentment. "Oh, Smoky...I still wish there was something I could do to thank you."

"You've already done it." Iampaatar gazed down

at the elderly woman. "You've helped me discover who I am, through all of these years. You've kept me clear on who I want to be. I'm dragon, always, first and foremost. But...you taught me what being human means. You've taught me to look outside of myself."

As she settled herself in his arms, he held her, kissing the strands of gray that covered her head. He could feel her life ebbing. She was tired, and so he whispered to her, "Sleep now. Sleep and dream, and move on."

Katja closed her eyes, lingering in the warmth of her dragon, and then, softly, she let go.

IAMPAATAR BURIED HER in the yard near her cabin, safely away where the scavengers couldn't find her. He tidied her place, making it ready for whoever might find it. The bow and arrows that she had carried, he took with him, mementoes of a brief time in his life that would forever stick with him.

As he shut the door behind him, he turned to look at the sky, toward the top of the world. His father was still there. He couldn't bring himself to go home, to face someone who stood for everything he hated. As he glanced over at the silent grave, he thought his mother was right. He liked mortals. He liked humans. Maybe it was time he tried his hand living among them. He'd go Earthside...find a place and settle down for a while. He was too restless to stay in the Northlands—it was too close to home.

So, he stepped back, and—changing into his magnificent dragon self—he rose into the air and headed toward the peaks that would take him into the world of humans. What he would find there, only the Hags of Fate knew. But Iampaatar—Smoky—had tasted the faint hints of what he thought might actually be love. And he knew that he wasn't going to find it with his betrothed. And love was something that he needed to have in his life.

Luck Be a Leprechaun

Bruce discovers the pitfalls of not being a stereotype. This story takes place at some point in late February after Panther Prowling.

BRUCE STARED AT the letter. He really, really didn't want to go home and tell Iris what it said because he knew it would provoke a blow up and he also knew there would be no getting out of the event. His mother would see to that. There is was, in front of him in black and white. Or rather, black on green. He'd been summoned to a Meet of the Southeastern Leprechauns Association and like it or not, he had to go. Iris could stew all she liked, and he was sure she would. But when the Duchess O'Shea personally phoned her son to insist he put in an appearance at an official event, there was nothing for it. He had to obey.

Sighing, he pulled on his blazer and made sure

he had everything he needed in his briefcase, and headed home for the night. He'd stop on the way to buy roses and candy and anything else he could think of to ease into breaking the news.

RATHER THAN TAKE a flight, Bruce made use of the portals. He had to first hop to Chicago, of all places, then to Tennessee, and stepped out of the portal near a Fae-run convenience store at the edge of the Monongahela National Forest, which lay deep in the Allegheny Mountains of West Virginia. The Meet was well within the forest, far away from civilization. He had hired a cab to take him to mile marker 5A, then paid the man and headed into the forest on foot.

Red spruce and hemlock were thick here, and poplar and white oak and rowan—or mountain ash, as it was called back in Washington State. Most of the trees were secondary forest. The woodlands had been logged off at one time and replanted, so most of them were the same age and size. The leaves were just budding into their spring greenery, the deciduous trees still looking sparse, their branches barely covered with the emerging hints of green.

As the fog rose thickly around him in the early morning, Bruce shivered. The forest was wet—wetter than Seattle, by far. No wonder it was known as *the birthplace of six rivers*. There was more than enough water here for a dozen rivers. As he tromped up the slope, he realized the undergrowth there wasn't quite the tangle it was at home, but the sight of the ferns and berries eased his mind. They were familiar.

Comfort shrubs, he thought with a laugh.

He had worn his windbreaker, and he had his pack with him. Iris had wanted him to take a friend—she had even suggested taking Vanzir or Rozurial, but Bruce could just imagine the furor if he showed up with one of the demon twins. Leprechaun society was notoriously tight-lipped, and it had taken long enough for him to convince his parents that he wasn't going to settle down with a nice leprechaun girl of nobility. He finally won them over to his lovely house-sprite, but it had taken awhile. Even the fact that she was a priestess of Undutar had failed to impress them. Finally, Bruce told them to suck it up and get over it.

So bringing a non-leprechaun to a Meet? *Not likely*. He was quite capable of hiking into it alone. He had a map, and by his computations, he should reach the meeting grounds by close to noon.

He stretched his arms, inhaling deeply. As he let out a slow stream of breath, his shoulders relaxed for the first time in months and he realized this might not be so bad. The twins were wonderful, and he loved being a husband and father, but he never could relax at home. Gods only knew how Iris felt—she was responsible for their care far more than he was.

If he was honest with himself, there were days he was grateful for having to go to the office. It got him away from the dirty diapers and the crying

and the constant need to be on alert. Even thinking about it made him feel guilty, and—as he gazed
around at his peaceful surroundings—it occurred
to him that he should invite his mother over for a
couple weeks and take Iris on vacation. She needed
it more than he did.

As he started off again, moving quickly up the
slope, it occurred to him that there might be wild
animals out here—ones who could easily make
a lunch off a leprechaun like himself. Or poison
oak...or poison ivy...or...

"Stop. You're working yourself up for nothing."

The sound of his voice was a sudden comfort.
Iris was right. He really *was* a city boy. *City leprechaun?* Whatever the case, Bruce was also the
first to admit that he wasn't comfortable out in
the wilds and he didn't care for roughing it. Iris
was much better suited toward camping, but then,
house sprites were—as a matter of course—hardier
and of solid stock compared to his own race. A
glance at his pocket watch told him he was about
three hours out from his destination, so he paused
to regroup, then started on again, trying to enjoy
the cool spring weather.

THREE HOURS LATER, and Bruce still hadn't
found the Meet. He was deep in the woods by now,
and tired and hungry, so he settled on a fallen log
to rest and eat. Iris had put up thick sandwiches
for him, along with cookies and a light, large bottle

of water, as well as other supplies. As he bit into the roast turkey, the silence of the forest slowly hit him. Oh, there was birdsong and the sound of water dripping off the trees, and all the various noises one expected in the woodland, but there was no buzz of power lines here, there were no sounds of traffic. He was truly alone.

Even more troubling was that he could detect no sounds of other leprechauns. His hearing was acute enough that he should hear something from the Meet by now. Finally, dreading what he had a feeling he was going to find, Bruce dragged out his map and tried to make heads or tails out of it. Iris had drilled him on it. She knew his shortcomings. Giving directions...and following them...were not among his strong points. But you'd think, being magical, the map would light up when he took a wrong turn.

As he tried to puzzle out which route he had taken, something on the corner of the map caught his eye and he groaned.

"*Fluffernuts*. I've been going the wrong direction all this time." He turned the map around and sure enough, the words flipped so they were readable no matter which way you positioned the map. And—*oh crap*, he hadn't bothered to check the compass. He'd assumed the top of the map was north, and the bottom was south.

"I'm a blathering idiot." Grumbling, he studied the map. Yes, instead of being at the Meet, he was now over *six* hours away from it. By the time he got there, it would be evening, and stumbling around in the woods in the dark wasn't an entirely safe thing to do. Pushing himself to his feet, he shouldered his pack, turned around and—making certain he was pointed in the right direction—he set off, hurrying as fast as he could without tripping himself up.

BY FIVE-THIRTY, the light was fading fast. The forest seemed to grow dim sooner than the cities. It was because of all the hills and vegetation getting in the way of the sun. He would soon be stumbling around in the dark, and there was still a good hour's walk before he made it to the Meet.

He leaned against one of the tall spruces, catching his breath, when the sound of voices caught his attention from a copse to the side. Squinting, he thought he saw a faint light through the trees. Relief spreading over him like a cool wave, he headed toward the noise. Either he had finally reached his destination, or he had found a group of campers. Either way, the thought of talking to someone other than a plant gave him comfort.

But as he broke through the brush, he saw a cabin. Old and weathered, it looked solidly made. Smoke rose from the chimney and soft lights glowed from inside. He scanned the area. There were no power lines and no sound of a generator, which probably meant the lights were kerosene or battery operated. Either way, it didn't matter to Bruce. Somebody was here, and that was enough. A battered pickup sat nearby, near a narrow dirt road to the east. This must be the drive to the main road. Bruce was tempted to ask for a ride to the closest town, where he could bag the Meet and just go home.

He knocked on the door. The voices inside fell silent and the next moment, a man as tall as Bruce was short yanked open the door. Well over six feet and burly, the man stared down at him. He had long hair caught back in a messy ponytail, and a beard that reached his chest. He wore dirty blue denim overalls. When he saw Bruce, his eyes lit up with an unnatural glint that made the leprechaun nervous.

Maybe I should have kept going after all.

The man cocked his head, staring at Bruce. "What do you want?"

"My name is Bruce O'Shea, and I seem to have lost my way out here—"

"Ma! Ma! You'll never believe what's on the porch." The man's voice echoed through the night, hale and hearty and a bit too excited for Bruce's comfort.

"What are you talking about, Rupert?" A woman's voice echoed from inside the cabin.

"A brownie—one of them sprites we heard about on the news!" The man reached down and—before Bruce could back away—caught him up around the waist and spun him around so he was inside the cabin. He set him down on the floor and pushed him forward. "Look, Ma! He showed up on the doorstep so he's ours, right? We can keep him?"

Bruce's ears perked up. *What the hell?* As he gazed around the cabin, it struck him that he maybe he slipped back in time, except for Rupert's comment about the news. The living room was spacious but sparse, with a ratty old sofa and armchair against one wall, a big woodstove to the right. A large table with six chairs sat near the opening to the kitchen. Two other doors led off to the right, and a ladder up to what looked to be a loft of sorts. The smell of stew wafted through the air, along with that of fresh bread. Bruce's stomach rumbled.

"Please, who are you?" Bruce managed to slip out of the man's grasp.

The mountain of a man stared down at him, alternately looking delighted and alarmed. "He can *talk*, Ma!"

Bruce backed up a step. Rupert didn't seem to be blessed in the brains department, and maybe it was better if he spent as little time here as possible. A noise from the kitchen startled him and he whirled to see a woman, thin and wiry, hustle out of the kitchen. She was wearing a floral housedress, over which she had tied a ruffled apron. Her hair, gray and fading rapidly into white, was caught back in a messy bun, and she looked exhausted.

"He's a tiny thing, ain't he?" She walked forward and leaned over, cocking her head. "What's your name, little fella?"

This conversation wasn't shaping up to be any better than the one with Rupert, but at least she was talking *to* him and not over his head.

"I'm Bruce O'Shea, and I was on my way to meet some friends for a...campout. I got lost. They should be close by. I thought at first that the light from your cabin was their campfire. I was obviously wrong, so I'll be going. Thank you, and I bid you good evening." He kept his voice as polite as possible, as he started to back away. But before he could make it to the door, he bumped into what felt like a tree trunk. As he turned around, Rupert stood there behind him, arms crossed, a cold smile on his face.

"Ma, the brownie doesn't want to stay. That's mighty unfriendly, don't you think?" Rupert reached down and clapped one meaty hand on Bruce's shoulder. "I thought brownies were supposed to be friendly and helpful."

"I'm not a brow—" Bruce started to say but the woman interrupted him.

"Yes, son, it is mighty unfriendly. Brownies are charitable folk, from what the TV show said, and you'd think he'd be a might more sociable, given he's in need of supper and a good place to stay. Maybe hunger is gnawing his gut and making him testy."

"Brownie? What makes you think I'm a brownie?" Bruce was feeling more confused by the minute, and the only thought that kept running through his head was, *"Get out of here now."*

"Of course you're a brownie. We've seen the shows. We saw Harry Potter in the theater. You're kin to that Dobby critter, aren't you?" The gleam in her eye grew stronger and Bruce began to sweat. "Now, Bruce—that your real name? Don't you have some fancy name we should know about? Some *secret* name?"

Bruce cleared his throat, thinking quickly. He decided it was better to lie than insist on the truth, at least until he knew what the hell was going on. "Secret name? Oh...sure! *Of course* I have a secret name. It's...it's..." His thoughts were blanking out, so he latched on the first thing that he could think of. Iris had been watching a lot of the Food Network lately, and they had recently watched *Lord of the Rings* again. "Altongorn Bobbigee."

The woman nodded wisely, touching the side of her nose. "Now we're getting somewhere. Well, Altongorn Bobbigee, you'll find us a fair family and we won't work you too hard, as long as you mind your manners. Now that we know your secret name, you won't be going anywhere, not until I give you permission. You belong to our household now. We can use a hand around here, that's for sure. Rupert, you go fetch the others to dinner. Altongorn—do you mind if I just call you by your given name?"

With the thought that he had just stumbled into his own Deliverance nightmare, Bruce swallowed. "Sure thing..."

"Good. Then, Altongorn, you put your pack over in that corner and help me set to dishing up supper. The boys and Flora will be mighty hungry."

Slipping his pack off his shoulders, Bruce contemplated making a run for it, but at that moment, Rupert bent down to whisper, "You're the best thing to happen to my Ma. If you so much as even *think* of running off, I'll bend you like an iron bar, and then take you apart, one limb at a time. Get the picture?"

Shuddering, Bruce nodded. He got the picture all right. He was stuck in a cabin full of backwoods folk who thought he was a brownie. And, for the moment, he was their prisoner.

AN HOUR LATER, the family was still eating, with Bruce relegated to a small table off to one side, a bowl of stew in front of him. Thank the gods it was venison and not something like possum. While he was sure possum was quite edible, and possibly tasty, he wasn't feeling much like taking any more chances.

The 'family' turned out to be four big boys, Flora—the daughter, and Ma—who told Bruce during the 'serving up' to call her Ellie Mae. She had been named after a TV character in an old TV comedy, although he wasn't sure which one and decided to refrain from asking. The boys were Rupert, Clive, Charles, and Hunker. Hunker's real name was Hank, but Hunker fit him. He skulked around with a hangdog look and Bruce had the feeling that he was the biggest brawn of the muscle boys.

After dinner, Ellie motioned for Bruce to follow her. He darted a longing look at the door, but the table, complete with the boys, stood between him and that lovely exit to freedom. With a long sigh, he entered the kitchen, staring at the pile of pans that were on the counter.

"You'll need this, Altongorn." Ellie held out a frilly white apron.

Bruce shook his head. "No thanks. I'm fine without it."

"Nonsense. You don't want to get those fancy clothes dirty while you're scrubbing pots. Take off your jacket and hold out your arms." She gave him a look that threatened violence if he refused so he slid out of his suit jacket—which had been beneath the Windbreaker—and held out his arms. She tied the apron around his waist. The bib was too long, as was the hem, but it would protect his clothes, that much she was right about.

As he stood there, he realized the kitchen had a door leading out to the back porch, and the back porch led to the woods. As he contemplated the likelihood of making it to the Meet without a flashlight, his map, or jacket, Ellie pulled a footstool over to the sink. Apparently, they had running cold water, but the hot water was steaming on the stove.

"I'll have Flora start bringing in the dishes." Ellie paused, then a sly grin stole over her face. "Mr. Brownie...I saw you checking out the door. Don't even think about making a run for the backside of the house. Wilson and Argo are out there. They're our guard dogs. They keep away the riffraff. And bears. And they haven't been fed tonight, if you get my drift." And with that, the older woman headed out of the room.

Bruce thought again about taking his chances but then a racket rose from behind the house—barking dogs who sounded like they were going batshit crazy—and he decided maybe it was better to lie low for the moment. He climbed on the footstool and, with a heavy heart, set to washing dishes.

Flora brought in all the bowls and the bread plate, handing them to him one by one as he dipped them in the hot soapy water and scrubbed them clean. Then, he rinsed them under cool running water and sat them in the drainer by the side of the sink. The soup pot was the hardest—it was huge and heavy, and by the time he was done, he was getting tired. Close to nine hours of hiking in the woods, then being hijacked by Hillbilly Central had left him irritated, worn out, and ready to bag this whole mess if he could figure out a way to sneak out of here.

When they were done, Flora motioned for him to follow her and they joined the others in the living room. Bruce was surprised to see Hunker reading, but as he looked closer, he realized that it was a survivalist's guide to making it through the coming apocalypse. Clive and Charles were playing a card game, and Rupert was in the rocking chair, staring at the woodstove, off in whatever La-La land he had concocted for himself. Ellie Mae was mending a dress. She glanced up as he followed Flora into the room.

"You get them dishes done, Altongorn?"

He nodded. "Yes, ma'am."

"Then have a seat by the fire and warm your toes."

As he sat down on a footstool near the welcoming flames, it occurred to him that his best bet would be to make an escape attempt after they were all in bed. But Ellie squashed that idea.

"We'll let you sleep in the utility closet. It's got space enough for a pallet and a warm quilt will set you up right nice. I gather your kind don't need as much in the way of space as we do?"

He could see it now, the lock on the outside of the door with only the darkness and spiders around him to keep him company. He had to put a stop to this before it got any worse.

"As I tried to tell you before, I'm not a brownie."

Rupert opened one eye. "But you're short, and you showed up on the doorstep right after Ma made a wish that she could get herself some help in the kitchen."

"Don't you people believe in coincidences?" Bruce let out a long sigh. "And a lot of people are short. I'm not a brownie, I'm a *leprechaun*. I have business to attend to, and I don't appreciate being locked up like a servant. I'm a professor at the University of Washington State."

Ellie squinted at him. "You live in the capital?"

"The other Washington—the *state*. I live in *Seattle*. I have a *wife and twins*. I have a *job*. I teach *Irish studies* at the university."

"Irish studies? You're Irish?" Flora cocked her head, a winsome smile crossing her face. Bruce was surprised they hadn't married her off yet.

He was feeling downright churlish now. "Hello... *leprechaun*? *Irish*? We kind of go together."

Clive decided to join the conversation. "If you're a leprechaun, where's that funny little hat you guys wear? The kind on the cereal commercial?"

"Yeah, and why aren't you dressed in green?" Rupert added.

"Where's your pot of gold? Say, if he *is* a leprechaun, he'll have a pot of gold at the end of the rainbow. We'll be rich! He has to give us wishes if he's really a leprechaun!" Charles was beaming. "Then, we can hire somebody to help out Ma."

"I still think he's a brownie. He's just lazy and trying to get out of an honest day's work. Just our luck, get stuck with a lazy brownie." Ellie Mae said. But, after a moment's deliberation, she squinted at Bruce. "If you're a leprechaun, then it's simple. We wait till the next rainy day—which'll likely be tomorrow—and then you find your rainbow and you give us your gold and we'll let you go back to wherever you came from." She gave a satisfied nod.

"No! It doesn't work that way. You're mixing up your mythologies with the actual facts—" Bruce tried to protest but they just began talking over him as if he weren't there, debating on what to do with his pot of gold once they took possession. He hunched closer to the stove. Could this *get* any worse?

"Then it's settled. Tomorrow, you give us your gold, we give you your freedom. Meanwhile, it's getting late. Time to turn in. Rupert, take Altongorn to the closet and make certain he has a blanket and something to cushion himself. We always take care of our guests." Ellie cleared her throat, indicating the conversation was over.

Rupert stood, staring down at Bruce. As Bruce reached for his pack, Rupert shook his head. "You can just leave that right there, Altongorn."

Following the behemoth of a man, Bruce swallowed a rising panic and let himself be shunted

into a dark, cramped closet. He managed to catch
sight of a few cobwebs before Rupert tossed in a
cushion just big enough to stretch out on, and then
a quilt. The door slammed shut and he heard a
lock turn.

Crap. Locked in. No doubt the place was crawl-
ing with spiders and maybe snakes. Probably
brown recluses, too. Maybe cottonmouths? While
poison affected the Fae differently than humans,
Bruce freely admitted he wasn't as brave as his
wife when it came to enemies. He'd happily face
down hellhounds and demons if it meant protect-
ing Iris or the twins, but for himself? Maybe not so
much.

Crouching on the cushion, he listened to the
voices outside the door. The utility closet had been
one of the rooms off the living room and within
ten minutes, the voices had faded to silence and he
realized everybody had gone to bed for the night.

The first order of business was to get some light
on the subject. He could conjure up light, and as
long as he maintained his control, it shouldn't be
so bright as to capture their attention. He coaxed
the flame to his hand—a green, pale flicker that
burned cool. Morio could charm the same type—
only the youkai-kitsune called it *foxfire*. Leprechauns called the flames *bog-lights*.

Once the light caught hold, he was able to look
around. The utility closet was about six by eight
feet, and it was filled with everything from a mop
and bucket, to a chainsaw and an axe. A hatchet
rested near the axe and as Bruce hefted it, he realized it was just the right size for him. Well, at least

he had a weapon. Apparently Ellie Mae and her family thought brownies—and leprechauns—didn't use weapons, which was good for him. Either that or they had forgotten about the blades being in here, a much more likely scenario.

Second order of business was quick and disappointing. He pulled out his cell phone to discover that—just as he thought—no bars. Shoving the phone back in his pocket, he considered his other options. Leprechaun magic was more geared toward magnetizing wealth, gold, money, and luck rather than toward defense or offense. And, unfortunately, he had no ability to contact anybody via any sort of telepathic powers.

For the first time in his life, Bruce wished he was something else. Even a human might be more capable of escaping than he was.

But...wait...He crouched by the door, aiming the light at the lock. A simple key lock. One thing he *had* learned was how to pick locks. Delilah had shown him one night when she was helping him watch the twins and Astrid—Chase's daughter. Iris and Camille were at the spa for some pampering, and Delilah had gotten bored. So she taught Bruce a couple judo moves and then they moved on to lock-picking.

While he didn't have a set of lock picks on him, he noticed that there were all sorts of tools lying around in the closet. He found a screwdriver, several pieces of metal wire, and a roll of electrical tape, among other things. He tucked the electrical tape in his pocket, then hunkered down. He'd wait another hour or so to give the Deliverance family plenty of time to get to sleep.

An hour passed, and he gave it twenty more minutes past that. Then, he quietly went to work at the lock, manipulating the tools cautiously. First, though, he positioned the quilt over beneath the door so that if he accidentally dropped anything, the sound of it would be cushioned by the material. But a couple hours later, when it was nearly midnight, his eyes started to close and he was nowhere near freeing himself. He was about to give it up for the night and go to sleep when he heard a sound outside the door. Quickly, he stuffed the tools beneath the blanket and curled up on the cushion, pretending to be asleep.

The door opened with a soft swish and the glow of a candle illuminated the room.

"Altongorn...Altongorn? Are you awake?" The voice was soft and feminine—it was Flora.

Bruce sat up, rubbing his eyes for effect. "Yes? What do you want?" He kept his voice low, not wanting to draw any unwanted attention if she had sneaked down on her own.

Flora motioned for him to come over to the door. "I was thinking...it's not right for you to be locked up like this. Ma needs the help but...they abolished slavery in the civil war, and even though you're a demon spawn, it's just not right."

Bruce blinked. Demon spawn? Well, whatever the case, she seemed sympathetic. "I have a family...they'll be missing me soon."

Flora nodded, then giggled softly and reached out to run her hand over his face. "You're a cute one, you know?"

Suddenly, Bruce wasn't feeling quite so chipper. The suggestive tone in her voice was a little too friendly. He cleared his throat. "Did I mention I'm married?"

"That don't bother me none. Half my boyfriends have been married too." The candle flame reflected in the gleam in her eye. "I can let you go, if you'll be nice to me."

Restraining a groan, Bruce tried to figure out what the hell to do. In the first place, he was married and he took his vows seriously. Secondly, he just wasn't interested in canoodling Flora. But if he could somehow manage to get out of here...

A thought struck him. "Listen, you're a very pretty girl. I'm sure I could be very nice to you, but if your brothers found us, my life would be on the line. They seem really protective of you."

She bit her lip. "Rupert busted Jimmy's arm two weeks ago when he caught us behind the barn. The bone broke right through the skin."

Repressing a shudder, Bruce nodded. "See? Maybe you could sneak us outside—make sure the dogs can't hear us and start up a racket. We could...have some fun in the barn?" He forced himself to push every hint of interest he could into his voice, then winked for good measure. He knew he was cute and he used it to his best effect here. Leprechauns didn't have quite the glamour that most of the Fae did, but they could wield a bit of charm, that was for certain.

Flora seemed to like the idea. She clapped her hands—then quickly stopped when Bruce held his finger to his lips. "Come with me. I can get us to the barn without the dogs noticing."

"I need my pack...there's...I have protection in there—and some...magical booze that will make it all that much more fun." He struggled with the lie. Iris always laughed at him when he tried to lie because he just wasn't good at it. But he wanted to make certain he had everything he'd need when he hightailed it out of here.

Flora squinted. "You sure it will make it even better? It usually feels pretty good without any help." She giggled and he had to stop himself from backing away.

"I know, but trust me. *Magic*, you know. Magic makes everything better."

She thought for a moment, then nodded. "Sure, Altongorn Bobbigee. What a funny name." As she let him out of the room and he tiptoed over to slip his pack over his shoulder, Flora motioned for him to follow her out the front door. There was a slight whimper from the back of the house but apparently the hounds were trained to focus on the kitchen door.

"The dogs are quiet," he said.

"Ma trained 'em to shut up except for what they're guarding. When they're tied out back, they guard the door there. Nobody ever would think of trying to come through our front door. My brothers have a reputation around these parts you know. One man tried to break in a couple years ago. He's buried over yonder, under that apple tree." She nodded to the side.

Bruce instantly brought his focus to bear. These folk didn't take kindly to anybody crossing their path, that was for certain. And he doubted that Flora would be all that happy when rejected her. He steeled himself, thinking he was going to have to do something he really didn't want to.

They reached the barn in a few minutes and she led him to an empty stall. It stunk to high heaven, a mixture of pig manure and dust and hay, but Bruce ignored the overwhelming odor as he planned out just how he was going to manage this.

Flora was arranging the straw, giggling a little more now. "I ain't never been with a brownie before." She turned to him. "But I'm willing to give anything a try at least once."

Bruce nodded, spying a sturdy chunk of wood near the entrance to the stall. Just what he needed. He pointed to the back corner. "You missed a spot there...might as well make the whole thing comfortable. We...brownies...can get pretty wild."

She brightened and handed him the candle. He set it down on the floor, away from the straw, and as she turned to spread more hay in the back, he grabbed the wood. He'd have one chance and one chance only. As he brought the wood down, praying he hadn't hit her too hard, she let out a little "O" and toppled forward.

Bruce quickly knelt beside her and felt for a pulse. She was still breathing, and her pulse felt rapid but safe. He quickly pulled the electrical tape out of his pocket and bound her hands behind her back. He then found a tie in his pack and gagged her. After that, he located a rope in the stall and fixed it so that she couldn't get out of the enclosure.

There. That would keep her till morning and since there were animals in the barn, he figured the boys would have to come feed them. They would find her then. In fact, he dragged her so she was near the opening. That way she could roll out enough to be seen by the time she woke up.

As soon as he made sure she was secured and firmly gagged, he blew out the candle, making certain the sparks were out. He frowned as he glanced down at Flora. Even though he felt bad for hitting her, he knew that she wouldn't have let him go. He also knew that her brothers would have ripped him to shreds if they even so much as suspected he touched her.

Quietly, he slipped out the barn. Thank heavens the clouds had broken and the moon was rising high over the forest. He glanced around, trying to pinpoint which way he had first approached the house. Within a few minutes, the moon cast her light on the path along which he had arrived. He had left his Windbreaker in the house, but there was no way in hell he was going back for it. Leaving the jacket, and his suit coat, behind, he slid the pack on his shoulders and took off into the night, with one last, nervous glance over his back.

AN HOUR LATER, he came to the Meet. The guards were patrolling the borders. As soon as they had identified him as Lord Bruce Golden Eagle O'Shea, the son of the Duke and Duchess O'Shea, he was in and safe.

When they asked him why he was late, he gave them a few choice words and ordered up some dinner. As he stretched out within the protection of the tent reserved for nobility, he thought about Ellie Mae and her family.

A weird sadness descended on him. Yes, they were scary, and probably dangerous, but Ellie Mae worked hard. And really, with the kids she had, what the hell was she *supposed* to do?

"Hey, Riley?" He motioned to one of the interns who was acting as a gofer.

"Yes milord?" Riley bowed, then handed Bruce a replacement suit coat. It didn't match his pants, but at least it would do for the general meetings, and he still had his formal dress with him.

"You know any out-of-work brownies around here?"

Riley blinked. "I might, milord. Why?"

Bruce laughed and leaned back, sipping the pint of ale. "I might have a job for one of them. Make sure it's a guy—I would never send a woman into this situation. Make certain he's cute, with a hearty appetite, and that he's smart enough to keep from getting caught if he likes to play chance with the ladies."

And with that, Bruce dismissed him. As he settled down for a long-overdue sleep, he made the decision that this would be the last Meet he would attend. If his mother wanted a family member to represent them so badly, she could send one of his brothers. And, he also decided, he would never, ever watch the movie *Deliverance* again.

Family Ties

Morio's family isn't quite as accepting as he's let on. This story takes place shortly after Panther Prowling.

"**ARE** YOU SURE you won't come? She wants to meet you." Morio was frustrated. Once again he was in an argument with his mother, and he knew he wouldn't win, but he had to try. That summed up their relationship: he did something she didn't like. He tried to convince her to cave. She guilt-tripped him into an apology.

A glance at the clock told him it was near dinner time. He made one more attempt. "I've told her that you accept her and our marriage. I told her that while you aren't thrilled about me marrying someone outside our people, you want me to be happy."

His mother's voice soared, and not in a pleasant

way. "You *know* our position. That you would lie to your wife, to the woman you married without our permission…this just shows me how far from the family honor you have fallen. You have no sense of decency anymore."

"I respect and love my family, Mother. I also respect and love my wife."

"Why you married her in the first place confounds us. Don't even start at me with your excuses. We know Grandmother Coyote ordered you to protect the girl. We accept that you must be involved with Camille and her sisters. But you were not required to involve yourself in her emotional life. You weren't forced to marry her. I can't even talk to my friends about this. I'd be a laughingstock. An unfit mother for letting her son stray so far from our traditions. Morio, you shame me—shameful, shameful son—"

And she was off again, ranting away. Morio let her whine without interrupting. He took the blame like he always did. If he had tried to defend himself, her tirade would have been worse, so might as well let her wind herself down. He was an old hand at wrangling his family.

Sure enough, a few minutes later, his mother changed the subject, and a few minutes later, she was ready to wrap things up.

"Your father and I are headed to dinner with the neighbors. They are going to introduce us to their granddaughter—she was just born. Their son is your age…" Yep, slip one last guilt-trip in for the road, and she was done. "You know we love you and just want what's best for you and the family."

And then...silence.

Morio slowly replaced the receiver. His mother always used a landline and never called cell phones. She insisted that if you were too busy to sit down and talk to her, she would just wait till you weren't distracted.

His grandfather was worse, detesting anything to do with technology or the humans who created it. Morio's father was silent on the subject, caught between *his* father's teachings, and a desire to understand his son.

Trouble was, Morio had fudged the truth to Camille. She thought they were okay with the marriage, but the truth was anything but that. His parents disliked and distrusted humans and Fae alike. When they found out he had married outside the clan, they had gone ballistic, threatening to come put an end to the union. It had taken every ounce of diplomacy he had to smooth things out so they weren't banging on the door with annulment papers. But he didn't want Camille to know that. It would hurt her feelings, terribly so. And the fact that his family lived in Japan made it much easier to put off the truth for now.

With a sigh, he headed for the kitchen. His monthly obligation was over till next time. Once more, he would lie and make up a bunch of general niceties to tell Camille and the others, while he just kept hoping that his parents would change their minds. Preferably sooner than later.

But an inner voice whispered, "*Fat chance...*" when he mused over the possibility.

A FEW DAYS later, the doorbell rang while he was playing a game of chess with Trillian. Morio was good, but the dark Fae— or dark elf, to be more precise—was a brilliant strategist. Morio had been practicing with him to better his skill.

Smoky answered. The girls were in the kitchen helping Hanna. Vanzir and Roz were at it with some video game again. A moment later, the dragon returned, a quizzical look on his face.

"Fox-boy, you better step outside for a minute."

"Oh?" Morio arched his eyebrows. By now what had begun as an insult was simply a nickname. "What's going on?"

"I advise doing so before Camille comes in asking who was at the door." Smoky's questioning look turned gloomy as he gave a warning shake of the head.

Frowning, Morio stood. A sudden sense of gloom swept past. Maybe it was because of the look on the dragon's face, or maybe it was an actual premonition, but a queasy wash hit the pit of his stomach. He cautiously headed toward the door, with Smoky behind him.

The wind was picking up as he stepped out onto the porch. Spring was around the corner, but it was still a ways off. The clouds were thick and black overhead. A thin sprinkle of rain started to spit down as Morio turned to see a spare figure standing next to the porch swing.

Crap. He knew that face, though it had been several years since he had seen the man.

"*Hayoto.* What are you doing here?"

While his cousin spoke perfect English, Morio switched over to Japanese just in case Hayoto said something that Morio didn't want the others to understand. Smoky might know the language, but there was a good chance nobody else in the household did. And the few rudimentary phrases he had taught Camille on her insistence were limited to ordering coffee, asking where the restroom was, and searching for the nearest magic shop.

Hayoto was dressed in dark jeans and a close-fit tailored shirt. He was the same age as Morio, but they had grown up wary, always on the outskirts of one another.

They competed in a way that neither could entirely understand, or even verbalize. Morio had always been a rebel. Hayoto had been the good son, much more judgmental. Both were intelligent, and neither welcomed interference in their lives. But when it came to family honor, Hayoto toed the line.

"Your mother asked me to check in on you." Hayoto's voice was cool. He neither hugged Morio, nor offered his hand.

Oh, lovely. His worst fears come to haunt him.

Morio frowned. "I didn't even realize you were in the country. When did you get here?"

"Two years ago. I moved to New York, but had to make a business trip to Seattle this week. My mother told your mother about the trip and so, here I am." He looked vaguely disapproving. "Your mother said you were messed up in the head."

That was about right. His mother would phrase it just like that. "There's no need. *Really*. My mother doesn't approve of my choices and she's pissed at me. This is no affair of yours."

"Anything to do with the family is my business. We have a responsibility to the clan." Hayoto scowled at him. "I'm getting married in a month, and she's a proper youkai. Whatever happened to *your* family loyalty?"

"I don't know what your problem is—I can't understand a word you two are saying, but I advise you to lower the volume right now." Smoky warned.

Seconds later, Camille popped her head out onto the porch. "What's going on? I heard voices—who's this?" She glanced at Hayoto, a curious look on her face.

Morio grimaced. He had hoped to get rid of Hayoto before he had to explain his presence, but now that idea was shot to hell.

"Meet Hayoto, my cousin." He turned to Hayoto. "My *wife*, Camille. And this is Smoky, he's part of our *quartet*. Camille is married to Smoky, me, and a dark Fae named Trillian."

"I knew you had crossed lines but I hadn't realized just how far you've fallen from honor. You break the boundaries and expect us to accept you and your...*consort*...with open arms?" Hayoto spoke in Japanese, but then turned to Camille and, in English, said, "So you are the cause of all the commotion."

"Commotion? What are you talking about?" Camille asked, a puzzled tone in her voice.

Morio winced. He would rather be anywhere else but here right now, at this moment. Even fighting demons seemed more pleasant. "I think I mentioned that not all of my family stands behind our marriage..."

Hayoto's cool smile turned to realization. "She doesn't know? Oh, this is rich. You turn your back on the family, then you lie to the woman you claim to love?"

Before Morio could stop him, Hayoto turned to Camille. "Morio's mother asked me to check in on him. He has disgraced our family by marrying you. He has broken tradition, refused to listen to reason, and has shattered his mother's heart."

Morio bristled. "How dare you talk to my wife that way—"

Camille let out a sharp cry, but before she could speak, Hayoto snorted and shook his head.

"The family will never recognize your marriage. I was also asked to deliver a message. Either you give up this charade and return home, or you will no longer be recognized by the Kuroyama clan." Hayoto folded his arms across his chest. "It's your true family, or this...*whore*."

Camille flew at him, but Smoky managed to catch her before she could do damage. He carried her inside and firmly shut the door. But Morio saw the hurt in her eyes. His heart thudded in his chest and though he wanted to wipe Hayoto's condescending smile off his face, he waited until the door closed to speak.

"If you think I will give up the woman I love, or the cause given to me by Grandmother Coyote, you've lost your mind. Also, know this: if you ever show up on my doorstep again, if you ever speak to my wife again, I will beat the living crap out of you. Then, I'll sic Smoky on you. And he happens to be a dragon. Now get out of here. You can tell my mother her plan backfired. Apparently, I'm no longer a member of the Kuroyama clan."

With one final contemptuous look, he turned his back on his cousin and hurried inside, slamming the door behind him.

THREE DAYS LATER, Camille still wasn't speaking to him. Morio had tried everything to get her to talk, but whenever he approached, she just gave him a hard stare and turned away.

Trillian finally cornered him after dinner. "Let me take you out for a drink. I think it would do her good to have an evening without you trying to patch things up. Right now, she just needs to work through her anger." He motioned to the door. "Come on."

Morio shrugged. "Might as well. The chill is biting around here, and I'm not talking about temperature. I don't blame her, though. I was such an idiot." He slipped on his leather jacket. "You want to drive?"

Trillian nodded. He'd recently got his license and was taking every opportunity to practice. "Let's head to the Shark Pit. If we go to the Wayfarer, Menolly will just run tales back to Camille." But he grinned as he said it.

Morio snorted. "Guess that's just the the pitfall

of having a sister-in-law who owns the best bar around. Every other place feels like a dive."

They headed to the Shark Pit, a dive run by Kek, a demon passing as Fae. Neither Morio nor Trillian knew exactly what kind of demon Kek was—Vanzir didn't even know and it wasn't good form to ask. But he was a good sort. He had fled the Sub-Realms when things started to go bad, and his joint served the low life of the Supe world. But he always made sure true troublemakers were kept out, and he wouldn't put up with anybody roughing up his customers.

The Shark Pit bore no resemblance to its name, having nothing to do with sharks, chum, or the water. It was a hole in the wall. A dimly lit tavern with a bar, four tables, one pool table, and a couple of video games. Food was simple: peanuts, pretzels and chips, and not the best quality on any of them.

Morio and Trillian managed to snag one of the tables. The customers came in to drink, not socialize, and for the most part, the regulars sat at the counter.

Kek meandered over, took one look at them and said, "Brandy?"

Trillian nodded. "Elfin, if you have it."

"Only for a price. We're down to our last bottle. It's dear now, given the destruction of Elqaneve. Going to be extremely pricey in a few months, so if you have any, I advise you to keep hold of it for investment purposes. I recommend you try Dream Weavers...made in Ceredream and pretty tasty. Even that will be dear, soon, given the fact that the City of the East has been trounced."

"At least they didn't get hit as bad as Elqaneve," Trillian said, pulling out his wallet. He tossed a twenty on the table. "Whatever that will buy."

"Four shots, and I'm being generous."

"That will do for a start." Trillian waved him off. He turned to Morio. "So, have you heard from your cousin again?"

Morio shook his head. "No, and I'm beginning to think I won't."

"You gave him an ultimatum, so you might not. Are you prepared for that?"

Morio had been asking himself that very thing. "What I hope for and what I'm likely to get are two different things. I should have just told Camille the truth in the first place, but I didn't want to hurt her feelings. With my family in Japan, I figured that I'd have time to bring them around to my side before they met."

He paused, gauging Trillian's reaction. The Svartan had similar problems when it came to in-laws. Camille's father had hated Trillian, and Trillian's family had written him off after he got involved with Camille. A real Romeo-Juliet sort of thing, only without so much death.

"How did you deal with your family? I know it didn't go well."

Trillian considered the question. He shrugged. "I never fit in anyway. I guess, for me, it was a matter of how much crap I was willing to take. I knew they would never accept Camille, and that left me with two choices: either stop seeing her, or walk away from my family. I figured that if they wouldn't accept the woman I loved, they could do without me.

So I left." His eyes were a shot of ice blue against the onyx of his skin and silver of his hair. He let out a snort. "Considering the only thing they held in hope for me was money, I decided I could do without their backing. Money's not *that* hard to come by."

"My family is so focused on honor and tradition. Our people—the youkai—are bound by all these rules and expectations passed down through the millennia. It's hard to turn my back on all of that. Kimiko, the nature spirit-goddess, personally looks after our family. I would be turning my back on her, too." But even as he said it, Morio knew his mind was already made up.

"You would be turning your back on Grand-mother Coyote if you let them sway you, and she's one of the Hags of Fate. HoF beats Nature Spirit any day." Trillian leaned back in his chair, eyeing the room. Weres lined the bar—it looked like some sort of bachelor party. "Face it, this life? It hasn't gone the way any of us expected it to. I wonder if it really ever does."

"Does what?"

"Does anybody ever reach the end of their life and think, *Wow...that went the way I thought it would—no detours, no abrupt turns, no forks in the road*?"

Morio grinned at him, finishing the second brandy. "Deep thoughts, bro. Deep thoughts."

"Always," Trillian countered, grinning. "I'll make a champion chess player of you, yet."

BY THE TIME they stumbled back to the car, Morio was mildly drunk. Trillian had stopped at drink number three, making certain he was good to drive. They sped through the silent streets. The nightlife in Seattle tended to congregate in buildings and stadiums, rather than in the middle of the streets. The ever present chill and rain that clouded the city most of the year saw to that.

As they pulled into the driveway, Morio frowned. The lights were blazing in the house—every light seemed to be on. The front door was open.

"What the hell?"

"I don't know. Let's find out." Trillian parked and they jogged over to where Vanzir was standing by the porch, scanning the yard.

"What's going on?" Morio barely got the words out before Vanzir jerked his head toward the door.

"You'd better get inside. Emergency."

"What the hell—" Morio lurched up the stairs. The warm buzz in his head began to fade as worry took over. Trillian followed him, punch sober.

The living room was a whirl. Nerissa was there, looking frantic, and Shade, who was frantically flipping through some sort of journal. Hanna was carrying a tea tray in, filled with tea and sandwiches. Roz was slipping on his duster—or rather, his portable armory.

"Where's Camille? Smoky?" Morio glanced around.

"Smoky's out at his barrow." Roz directed the

two of them to the sofa. "Your cousin showed up tonight after you left."

Uh oh. That can't be good, Morio thought. "What did he want?"

"He wanted to talk to Camille. He was browbeating her, trying to convince her to let you go."

Morio growled. "I'll beat the living hell out of him."

"She already started. Or rather, she was giving him an earful—and you do not want to know what kind of language she was using—but by the time she finished, she had backed him outside to the porch. I was starting to follow, I didn't want her out there alone with him, when the wards went off. I rushed out in time to see Camille racing for the backyard. Hayoto was following her. I came back in to grab my coat here."

"It's a demon on the land." Shade looked up from his notebook. "But I can't tell you what kind, though it's probably a bloatworgle."

Roz nodded. "We don't know where they went. I was about to head out to find her, but Vanzir said you were pulling in so I decided to wait."

A bloatworgle. Bloated and putrid, the demons were nasty, and they could breathe fire. They also could gut a cow with one swipe of their long, taloned claws.

The alcohol fled from Morio's body in a rush of adrenaline—one of the perks of being a youkai. "I'm on my way. You said toward the back?"

"We think it came in through the rogue portal on the land." Shade turned around, a serious look on his face. "Delilah is on her way home from her martial arts program. I called Menolly and she'll be home as soon as she can make sure the bar's covered."

"We don't have time to wait. Come on." Morio turned to Trillian. "Let's go. Roz, you head toward the pond, just in case they went that way. Vanzir, stay here and guard the house with Shade."

Trillian was headed toward the utility room where they kept spare weapons. "Let me grab a weapon. You need one?"

"I *am* one." His expression grim, Morio headed for the kitchen door.

BACKYARD WAS A misnomer. Stretching out for close to fifteen acres, the land stretched into forest and wetlands, and eventually came to Birchwater Pond. The rogue portal lie west of the pond, through what had been a stand of tall grass until the guys had built Iris and Bruce's house.

One of the few places the house could be easily placed, it meant that Iris had a rogue portal basically across the street from her. She wasn't thrilled about the idea, but there was no help for it. During the autumn before, they had laid a sidewalk from the main house to Iris's place.

The thought had first been to use cobblestones, but even though they were pretty, the face of the stones was incredibly slick during the rainy season, and the mold grew faster than it could be power washed away. It was just part and parcel of living in the NW. Mold made streets slick. Mud made paths both nasty and slick. So they opted for a simple concrete sidewalk, wide enough for a wheelbarrow, strollers, and whatever else might be needed. The sidewalk was wet, but it was clean of debris as Morio raced along it, Trillian close on his heels.

As they passed Iris's house, it was lit up, and Chase was standing guard at the front porch.

Morio paused. "Did you see them go by?"

"Yeah. We have a warding system set up here too. When it went off I came out to see what was going on. Camille and some strange man went racing past. Iris is alone with the babies or I would have gone after them. Bruce is at a meeting at the UW tonight."

"Which way did they go?"

"Camille headed off over toward the Standing Tree." Chase pointed to one of the trees. They'd nicknamed it the Standing Tree because it had a double trunk, looking for all the world like a man standing with spread legs. "The guy who was with her followed her into the brush."

Morio started out at a dead run again, with Trillian right behind him. Behind him, Chase said something but neither managed to catch what it was.

The night closed in around them as they plunged into the eight-foot tall patch of Scotch broom that led to the rogue portal. A rough path had been carved through the gorse, thanks to the guards from Talamh Lonrach Oll. But obviously, somebody was off their game tonight, because there were no guards in sight.

Rounding a curve, Morio skidded to a stop. Up ahead, the portal shimmered between two trees. Near it, he could see Camille—she was building energy, that much he could tell, drawing it down from the hidden moon overhead. To her left, stood the bloatworgle, one gorilla-like arm holding Hayoto by the collar. Hayoto was unconscious...if he was still alive at all.

The bloatworgle let out a roar but Camille stood her ground.

Morio began to shift into his demonic form, but as he was in mid-transformation, the bloatworgle brought Hayoto's hand up to his mouth, about to bite down.

"No you don't!" Camille launched a bolt of energy in the demon's direction. The bloatworgle roared, shooting a mouthful of fire toward the Moon witch.

Trillian leaped toward her, but the fire caught her full force before he could reach her side. She screamed as flames licked at her gown, sending wisps of smoke up as the material began to spark and sputter.

Horrified, Morio waded in, smashing at the demon. The bloatworgle dropped Hayoto and turned toward him. Fully eight feet tall and terrifying in his demonic fury, Morio caught the creature full force with a blow to the head. The demon lurched back, but came at him again.

The bloatworgle opened his mouth to send a breath of fire but, once again, Morio slammed his fist into the creature's face. He grabbed the bloatworgle by the neck and squeezed.

The demon slashed out with his long talons, clipping Morio across the chest. Blood began to seep from the gash marks lining his torso, but the sear of pain only drove the youkai-kitsune's fury on.

The sight of Camille, burned and weeping, as Trillian cautiously moved her out of the way...the sight of his cousin prone on the ground...it was all enough to send Morio over the edge. He whirled on the bloatworgle, in a frenzy of anger, slashing with his own claws. Blood sprayed through the air. Once again, Morio let go with a right hook that caught the creature under the chin. An audible crack split the air, as the bloatworgle landed on the ground.

Morio leaped, landing square atop him, his meaty fists coming down. He dug deep with his claws, eviscerating the bloatworgle. The demon groaned and clutched his belly, a short burst of flame flaring out of his mouth as he let loose one last shriek and fell silent.

With one last glance at the portal to make certain no more followed the first, Morio quietly shifted back to his human form and ran to Camille's side.

Trillian was cradling her in his arms. Several large blisters had formed on her skin, but he had managed to strip off the smoldering clothing before a painful injury could become life-threatening.

"She's going to have a few scars and hurt like hell for a couple weeks, but if we get her back to the house now, she should be all right, I think."

Trillian glanced at Morio. "You should shift back into youkai form. You can carry her easier. I'll see to your cousin."

Morio nodded. Once again, he transformed. Gently lifting Camille into his arms, he winced as she let out a moan. Without another word, he began to quickly, smoothly, lope back to the house.

IRIS HAD HUSTLED up to take care of Camille, leaving Chase to watch the babies. She and Hanna were laying out their ointments and salves, arguing over what would be best to use. Vanzir headed back to the rogue portal to find out what had happened to the guards and make certain no stray sparks from the bloatworgle had started any fires.

Hanna finally agreed to tend to Hayoto, while Iris undressed Camille and examined her wounds.

"She'll live, but she's going to be in a world of hurt while she mends. But these aren't serious enough for us to send for the medic. She's lucky you were there to pull the burning cloth away from her. Somebody fill the bathtub. Make certain the water is cool, but not cold. Slightly cooler than lukewarm, but no more. And I need some antibiotic soap." Iris motioned to Morio. "Carry her to the bathroom when the tub is ready. Gently—very gently—lower her into the tub."

"I hurt like a son of a bitch," Camille moaned, trying to sit up.

Iris pushed her back. "Hush. You lie down and

let me look you over. All the damage appears to be on your front side."

"That's because I was facing the bloatworgle. Thank gods I had my hair back in a ponytail." She let out a gasp and winced again. "Damn, this hurts."

"How's Hayoto?" Morio turned to Hanna.

"He'll be all right. Looks like he was knocked unconscious but his eyes are beginning to flicker and I don't see any obvious bumps or lumps."

"He's lucky he still has his hand." Morio gritted his teeth as he lifted Camille and carried her into the downstairs bathroom. At that moment, the front door opened and Delilah rushed through. She was panting.

"I got stuck in traffic. What happened?" She spied Camille and let out a gasp. "What the hell—"

"Walk and talk, woman." Iris bustled past. "Morio, get her in the tub. I'm going to get some clean sheets and arrange them on the sofa. Nerissa, you go tell Chase I'll be staying up here tonight to keep an eye on things. I'll pump some breast milk while I'm waiting and you can take it down for him to feed the babies. He's good at that."

Nerissa nodded, heading out the door. Nobody messed with Iris when she took control.

Once Camille's wounds were clean—and the soot was washed away—Iris slathered her burns with a thin layer of salve and then loosely bandaged the open blisters with light gauze. After they settled Camille on the sofa, Hanna brought her a cup of charyo tea, a powerful pain reliever.

"What happened out there?" Morio sat down by

her side.

"Your cousin and I were arguing on the porch. The wards went off and I could feel the bloatworgle. Well, I didn't know it was a bloatworgle at the time, but I could feel Demonkin near." She paused to shift position, wincing as she did so. "I headed to the portal and your cousin followed. He was yammering in my ear, asking what the hell was going on, when the bloatworgle jumped out from behind a bush and smacked him over the head. It was going to kill him, so I body slammed the thing and drew its attention. The bloatworgle and I got into it, but as I was regrouping, summoning up the Moon Mother's energy, the demon grabbed hold of your cousin and tried to drag him off. That's when you showed up."

Morio nodded. He was about to go check on his cousin when a voice interrupted from the entrance to the living room.

"She saved my life out there." Hayoto was leaning against the archway. "I was still conscious after that first blow and I saw what it was about to do to me. Your...wife...risked her own life to save me." He flickered his gaze over to Camille, then to the floor. "I cannot imagine why you would bother, when I was so cruel to you."

"You're my husband's cousin. We place a high value on family, dude. Even if family turns its back on us." Camille's tone was stony, but Morio knew just how much it cost her to say that. Her own father had disowned her for a time, and they had only begun to repair the rift when he died in the destruction of Elqaneve.

Morio turned to Hayoto. "Now you see why this woman...*these people*...are my family. If you still don't approve, then leave here and never darken our door again. You can report back to my mother than I'm a lost cause. At least I'm lost on the right side."

Hayoto shook his head. "I won't be telling her that." He turned to Camille. "My actions...my words...were inexcusable. I don't expect you to accept my apology, but please, know that I mean every word of it. I was judgmental where I had no right to be, and I made assumptions I had no right to make. I'd like to call you cousin, if I may?"

Camille stared at his outstretched hand. The look in his eyes said far more than his words, and she placed her hand in his.

"Apology accepted. But you have to promise to stay with us for a couple days and truly get to know us. And you have to buy us ice cream. Lots of ice cream. And coffee. Lots of coffee. That is, if Morio agrees. It's *his* decision. He's the one you wronged the most."

Laughing, Hayoto nodded. He turned to Morio. "My apology to you...goes beyond words. I am afraid to ask but...are we are still cousins?"

Morio let out a long breath. It would be an uphill battle with his parents, but with Hayoto's help, there might be hope. And hope...hope was their mainstay right now.

"Cousins...yes. Family. Now sit down. That blow to the head wasn't an easy one. Speaking of ice cream, if Menolly's still on the way, can somebody call her and ask her to pick some up? Nothing's too good for my wife."

Morio glanced around the room. The journey from Japan to the living room in Belles-Faire had a been a long and winding one, but he realized that he was truly home. This house, these people, they were his life and his family. And family was what mattered the most.

If you enjoyed this book, know that the most recent Otherworld book—MOON SHIMMERS—was just released. The next Otherworld book—HARVEST SONG—will be out May 2018.

Meanwhile, how about getting acquainted with my new characters—the wild and magical residents of Bedlam in my Bewitching Bedlam Series, about fun-loving witch Maddy Gallowglass, her smoking-hot vampire lover, and their crazed cjinn Bubba (part djinn, all cat). Read BLOOD MUSIC, the prequel, and BEWITCHING BEDLAM—the first in the series, while waiting for MAUDLIN'S MAYHEM to come out.

Or, if you prefer a grittier series, try my post-apocalyptic paranormal romance—the Fury Unbound Series. The first two books—FURY RISING and FURY'S MAGIC—are out, and the third will be out in June 2017.

You can also read my entire Chintz 'n China paranormal mystery series, including HOLIDAY SPIRITS, the holiday novella I wrote to wrap it up.

For all of my work, see the Bibliography at the end of this book, or check out my website at Galenorn.com and be sure and sign up for my newsletter to receive news about all my new releases.

Upcoming releases

June 2017: Fury Awakened (Fury Unbound—Book 3)
July 2017: Maudlin's Mayhem (Bewitching Bedlam—Book 2)
August 2017: Fury Calling (Fury Unbound—Book 4)
October 2017: Siren Song (Bewitching Bedlam—Book 4)
October 2017: Taming the Shifter (Anthology)
November 2017: Fury's Mantle (Fury Unbound—Book 5)
December 2017: Silent Night (Otherworld Holiday Novella)

Cast of Major Characters

The D'Artigo Family:

Arial Lianan te Maria: Delilah's twin who died at birth. Half-Fae, half-human.

Camille Sepharial te Maria, aka Camille D'Artigo: The oldest sister; a Moon Witch and Priestess. Half-Fae, half-human.

Daniel George Fredericks: The D'Artigo sisters' half cousin; FBH.

Delilah Maria te Maria, aka Delilah D'Artigo: The middle sister; a werecat.

Hester Lou Fredericks: The D'Artigo sisters' half cousin; FBH.

Maria D'Artigo: The D'Artigo Sisters' mother. Human. Deceased.

Menolly Rosabelle te Maria, aka Menolly D'Artigo: The youngest sister; a vampire and *jian-tu:* extraordinary acrobat. Half-Fae, half-human.

Sephreh ob Tanu: The D'Artigo Sisters' father. Full Fae. Deceased.

Shamas ob Olanda: The D'Artigo girls' cousin. Full Fae. Deceased.

The D'Artigo Sisters' Lovers & Close Friends:

Astrid (Johnson): Chase and Sharah's baby daughter.

Bruce O'Shea: Iris's husband. Leprechaun.

Carter: Leader of the Demonica Vacana Society, a group that watches and records the interactions of Demonkin and human through the ages. Carter is half demon and half Titan—his father was Hyperion, one of the Greek Titans.

Chase Garden Johnson: Detective, director of the Faerie-

Human Crime Scene Investigation (FH-CSI) team. Human who has taken the Nectar of Life, which extends his life span beyond any ordinary mortal and has opened up his psychic abilities.

Chrysandra: Waitress at the Wayfarer Bar & Grill. Human. Deceased.

Derrick Means: Bartender at the Wayfarer Bar & Grill. Werebadger.

Erin Mathews: Former president of the Faerie Watchers Club and former owner of the Scarlet Harlot Boutique. Turned into a vampire by Menolly, her sire, moments before her death. Human.

Greta: Leader of the Death Maidens; Delilah's tutor.

Iris (Kuusi) O'Shea: Friend and companion of the girls. Priestess of Undutar. Talon-haltija (Finnish house sprite).

Lindsey Katharine Cartridge: Director of the Green Goddess Women's Shelter. Pagan and witch. Human.

Maria O'Shea: Iris and Bruce's baby daughter.

Marion Vespa: Coyote shifter; owner of the Supe-Urban Café.

Morio Kuroyama: One of Camille's lovers and husbands. Essentially the grandson of Grandmother Coyote. Youkai-kitsune (roughly translated: Japanese fox demon).

Nerissa Shale: Menolly's wife. Worked for DSHS. Now working for Chase Johnson as a victims-rights counselor for the FH-CSI. Werepuma and member of the Rainier Puma Pride.

Roman: Ancient vampire; son of Blood Wyne, Queen of the Crimson Veil. Menolly's official consort in the Vampire Nation and her new sire.

Queen Asteria: The former Elfin Queen. Deceased.

Queen Sharah: Was an elfin medic, now the new Elfin Queen; Chase's girlfriend.

Rozurial, aka Roz: Mercenary. Menolly's secondary lover. Incubus who used to be Fae before Zeus and Hera destroyed his marriage.

Shade: Delilah's fiancé. Part Stradolan, part black (shadow) dragon.

Siobhan Morgan: One of the girls' friends. Selkie (wereseal); member of the Puget Sound Harbor Seal Pod.

Smoky: One of Camille's lovers and husbands. Half-white, half-silver dragon.

Tanne Baum: One of the Black Forest Woodland Fae. A member of the Hunter's Glen Clan.

Tavah: Guardian of the portal at the Wayfarer Bar & Grill. Vampire (full Fae).

Tim Winthrop, aka Cleo Blanco: Computer student/genius, female impersonator. FBH. Now owns the Scarlet Harlot.

Trillian: Mercenary. Camille's alpha lover and one of her three husbands. Svartan (one of the Charming Fae).

Ukkonen O'Shea: Iris and Bruce's baby son.

Vanzir: Was indentured slave to the Sisters, by his own choice. Dream-chaser demon who lost his powers and now is regaining new ones.

Venus the Moon Child: Former shaman of the Rainier Puma Pride. Werepuma. One of the Keraastar Knights.

Wade Stevens: President of Vampires Anonymous. Vampire (human).

Zachary Lyonnesse: Former member of the Rainier Puma Pride Council of Elders. Werepuma living in Otherworld.

Glossary

Black Unicorn/Black Beast: Father of the Dahns unicorns, a magical unicorn that is reborn like the phoenix and lives in Darkynwyrd and Thistlewyd Deep. Raven Mother is his consort, and he is more a force of nature than a unicorn.
Calouk: The rough, common dialect used by a number of Otherworld inhabitants.
Court and Crown: "Crown" refers to the Queen of Y'Elestrial. "Court" refers to the nobility and military personnel that surround the Queen. "Court and Crown" together refer to the entire government of Y'Elestrial.
Court of the Three Queens: The newly risen Court of the three Earthside Fae Queens: Titania, the Fae Queen of Light and Morning; Morgaine, the half-Fae Queen of Dusk and Twilight; and Aeval, the Fae Queen of Shadow and Night.
Crypto: One of the Cryptozoid races. Cryptos include creatures out of legend that are not technically of the Fae races: gargoyles, unicorns, gryphons, chimeras, and so on. Most primarily inhabit Otherworld, but some have Earthside cousins.
Demon Gate: A gate through which demons may be summoned by a powerful sorcerer or necromancer.
Demonica Vacana Society: A society run by a number of ancient entities, including Carter, who study and record the history of demonic activity over Earthside. The archives of the society are found in the Demonica Catacombs, deep within an uninhabited island of the Cyclades, a group of Grecian islands in the Aegean Sea.
Dreyerie: A dragon lair.
Earthside: Everything that exists on the Earth side of the portals.
Elqaneve: The Elfin city in Otherworld, located in

Kelvashan—the Elfin lands.

Elemental Lords: The elemental beings—both male and female—who, along with the Hags of Fate and the Harvestmen, are the only true Immortals. They are avatars of various elements and energies, and they inhabit all realms. They do as they will and seldom concern themselves with humankind or Fae unless summoned. If asked for help, they often exact steep prices in return. The Elemental Lords are not concerned with balance like the Hags of Fate.

FBH: Full-Blooded Human (usually refers to Earthside humans).

FH-CSI: The Faerie–Human Crime Scene Investigation team. The brainchild of Detective Chase Johnson, it was first formed as a collaboration between the OIA and the Seattle police department. Other FH-CSI units have been created around the country, based on the Seattle prototype. The FH-CSI takes care of both medical and criminal emergencies involving visitors from Otherworld.

Great Divide: A time of immense turmoil when the Elemental Lords and some of the High Court of Fae decided to rip apart the worlds. Until then, the Fae existed primarily on Earth, their lives and worlds mingling with those of humans. The Great Divide tore everything asunder, splitting off another dimension, which became Otherworld. At that time, the Twin Courts of Fae were disbanded and their queens and the Merlin were stripped of power. This was the time during which the Spirit Seal was formed and broken in order to seal off the realms from each other. Some Fae chose to stay Earthside, others moved to the realm of Otherworld, and the demons were—for the most part—sealed in the Subterranean Realms.

Guard Des'Estar: The military of Y'Elestrial.

Hags of Fates: The women of destiny who keep the balance righted. Neither good nor evil, they observe the flow of destiny. When events get too far out of balance, they step in and take action, usually using humans, Fae, Supes, and other creatures as pawns to bring the path of destiny back into line.

Harvestmen: The lords of death—a few cross over and

are also Elemental Lords. The Harvestmen, along with their followers (the Valkyries and the Death Maidens, for example), reap the souls of the dead.

Haseofon: The abode of the Death Maidens—where they stay and where they train.

Ionyc Lands: The astral, etheric, and spirit realms, along with several other lesser-known noncorporeal dimensions, form the Ionyc Lands. These realms are separated by the Ionyc Seas, a current of energy that prevents the Ionyc Lands from colliding, thereby sparking off an explosion of universal proportions.

Ionyc Seas: The currents of energy that separate the Ionyc Lands. Certain creatures, especially those connected with the elemental energies of ice, snow, and wind, can travel through the Ionyc Seas without protection.

Kelvashan: The lands of the elves.

Koyanni: The coyote shifters who took an evil path away from the Great Coyote; followers of Nukpana.

Melosealfôr: A rare Crypto dialect learned by powerful Cryptos and all Moon Witches.

The Nectar of Life: An elixir that can extend the life span of humans to nearly the length of a Fae's years. Highly prized and cautiously used. Can drive someone insane if he or she doesn't have the emotional capacity to handle the changes incurred.

Oblition: The act of a Death Maiden sucking the soul out of one of their targets.

OIA: The Otherworld Intelligence Agency; the "brains" behind the Guard Des'Estar. Earthside Division now run by Camille, Menolly, and Delilah.

Otherworld/OW: The human term for the "United Nations" of Faerie Land. A dimension apart from ours that contains creatures from legend and lore, pathways to the gods, and various other places, such as Olympus. Otherworld's actual name varies among the differing dialects of the many races of Cryptos and Fae.

Portal, Portals: The interdimensional gates that connect the different realms. Some were created during the Great Divide; others open up randomly.

Seelie Court: The Earthside Fae Court of Light and

Summer, disbanded during the Great Divide. Titania was the Seelie Queen.

Soul Statues: In Otherworld, small figurines created for the Fae of certain races and magically linked with the baby. These figurines reside in family shrines and when one of the Fae dies, their soul statue shatters. In Menolly's case, when she was reborn as a vampire, her soul statue re-formed, although twisted. If a family member disappears, his or her family can always tell if their loved one is alive or dead if they have access to the soul statue.

Spirit Seals: A magical crystal artifact, the Spirit Seal was created during the Great Divide. When the portals were sealed, the Spirit Seal was broken into nine gems and each piece was given to an Elemental Lord or Lady. These gems each have varying powers. Even possessing one of the spirit seals can allow the wielder to weaken the portals that divide Otherworld, Earthside, and the Subterranean Realms. If all of the seals are joined together again, then all of the portals will open.

Stradolan: A being who can walk between worlds, who can walk through the shadows, using them as a method of transportation.

Supe/Supes: Short for Supernaturals. Refers to Earthside supernatural beings who are not of Fae nature. Refers to Weres, especially.

Talamh Lonrach Oll: The name for the Earthside Sovereign Fae Nation.

Triple Threat: Camille's nickname for the newly risen three Earthside Queens of Fae.

Unseelie Court: The Earthside Fae Court of Shadow and Winter, disbanded during the Great Divide. Aeval was the Unseelie Queen.

VA/Vampires Anonymous: The Earthside group started by Wade Stevens, a vampire who was a psychiatrist during life. The group is focused on helping newly born vampires adjust to their new state of existence, and to encourage vampires to avoid harming the innocent as much as possible. The VA is vying for control. Their goal is to rule the vampires of the United States and to set up an internal policing agency.

Whispering Mirror: A magical communications device

that links Otherworld and Earth. Think magical video phone.

Y'Eírialiastar: The Sidhe/Fae name for Otherworld.

Y'Elestrial: The city-state in Otherworld where the D'Artigo girls were born and raised. A Fae city, recently embroiled in a civil war between the drug-crazed tyrannical Queen Lethesanar and her more level-headed sister Tanaquar, who managed to claim the throne for herself. The civil war has ended and Tanaquar is restoring order to the land.

Youkai: Loosely (very loosely) translated as Japanese demon/nature spirit. For the purposes of this series, the youkai have three shapes: the animal, the human form, and the true demon form. Unlike the demons of the Subterranean Realms, youkai are not necessarily evil by nature.

Biography

New York Times, *Publishers Weekly*, and *USA Today* bestselling author Yasmine Galenorn writes urban fantasy and paranormal romance, and is the author of over fifty books, including the Otherworld Series, the Whisper Hollow Series, the Fury Unbound Series, the upcoming Bewitching Bedlam Series, and many more. She's also written nonfiction metaphysical books. She is the 2011 Career Achievement Award Winner in Urban Fantasy, given by RT Magazine.

Yasmine has been in the Craft since 1980, is a shamanic witch and High Priestess. She describes her life as a blend of teacups and tattoos. She lives in Kirkland, WA, with her husband Samwise and their cats. Yasmine can be reached via her web site at Galenorn.com.

Books by Yasmine Galenorn:

Fury Unbound Series:
Fury Rising
Fury's Magic
Fury Awakened (June 2017)
Fury Calling (August 2017)
Fury's Mantle (November 2017)
Fury Unchained (2018)

Bewitching Bedlam Series:
Blood Music (Prequel novelette)
Bewitching Bedlam
Maudlin's Mayhem (July 2017)
Siren's Song (October 2017)
Witches Wild (2018)

Otherworld Series (in order):
Witchling
Changeling
Darkling
Dragon Wytch
Night Huntress
Demon Mistress
Bone Magic
Harvest Hunting
Blood Wyne
Courting Darkness
Shaded Vision
Shadow Rising
Haunted Moon
Autumn Whispers
Crimson Veil
Priestess Dreaming
Panther Prowling
Darkness Raging
Moon Shimmers
Harvest Song (2018)
Blood Bonds (2019)

Otherworld: E-Novellas:
The Shadow of Mist: Otherworld novella
Etched in Silver: Otherworld novella
Ice Shards: Otherworld novella
Flight From Hell: Otherworld--Fly By Night crossover
novella
Earthbound
Silent Night: Otherworld Holiday Novella (December
2017)

Otherworld: Short Collections:
Otherworld Tales: Volume One
Tales From Otherworld: Collection One
Men of Otherworld: Collection One
Men of Otherworld: Collection Two
Moon Swept: Otherworld Tales of First Love

Chintz 'n China Series:

Ghost of a Chance
Legend of the Jade Dragon
Murder Under a Mystic Moon
A Harvest of Bones
One Hex of a Wedding
Holiday Spirits

Whisper Hollow Series (in order):
Autumn Thorns
Shadow Silence

Lily Bound Series (in order):
Souljacker

Fly By Night Series (in order):
Flight from Death
Flight from Mayhem

Indigo Court Series (in order):
Night Myst
Night Veil
Night Seeker
Night Vision
Night's End

Indigo Court: Novellas:
Night Shivers

Bath and Body Series (originally under the name India Ink):
Scent to Her Grave
A Blush With Death
Glossed and Found

Misc. Short Story Collections:
Mist and Shadows: Short Tales From Dark Haunts

Anthologies:
Winter's Heat (novelette: Blood Vengeance)
Taming the Shifter (novelette: Tiger Tails)
Once Upon a Kiss (short story: Princess Charming)
Silver Belles (short story: The Longest Night)

Once Upon a Curse (short story: Bones)
Never After (Otherworld novella: The Shadow of Mist)
Inked (Otherworld novella: Etched in Silver)
Hexed (Otherworld novella: Ice Shards)
Songs of Love & Death (short story: Man in the Mirror)
Songs of Love and Darkness (short story: Man in the Mirror)
Nyx in the House of Night (article: She is Goddess)
A Second Helping of Murder (recipe: Clam Chowder)

Magickal Nonfiction:
From Llewellyn Publications and Ten Speed Press:
Trancing the Witch's Wheel
Embracing the Moon
Dancing with the Sun
Tarot Journeys
Crafting the Body Divine
Sexual Ecstasy and the Divine
Totem Magic
Magical Meditations

Made in the USA
Columbia, SC
16 January 2018